She Fell in love With A Dope Boy 4

Miss Candice

Published by Leo Sullivan Presents

Recap

After seeing what I saw last night, I forced myself to go to sleep. I couldn't stay up. It would be the only thing I thought about. I needed to shut my mind off. I needed to rejuvenate myself too. I slept long and hard. When I did finally wake up, I had three missed calls from Sinn. I couldn't understand why she was hitting me up when I'm quite sure she knows that Cassim... that Cassim and I were taking a break.

That's what I'll call it. Taking a break. All I needed was five minutes with him. All I needed was to grab a hold of his hand. All he needed was to hear my sincerest apology. We could move past this right? We had to. For the sake of my sanity, we had to.

I sat up and rested up against the headboard to call Sinn back.

"Whew! Thank God you still alive. Bitch, I was about to ride out looking for—"

"What's up, Sinn," I said, cutting the dramatics short.

"What's up with you and Cass?"

I frowned, "What? Why?"

"Something is off. I already know something is off. That nigga has been buggin out for the last few days. Do you know he forced my man to play Russian Roulette with him last night? He put a gun to my man's head and told him if he didn't play he would pull the trigger. Na, I love Cass, but I'd be damned if—"

"Where is he," I asked with wide eyes.

"In my basement passed out," she said with an attitude. "Na, Luck told me that something happened between you two, but he didn't know what."

"Is it okay if I come by?"

She paused, "I don't know, Ryann. Nate is here, and I really don't want any drama going on in front of him."

I shook my head, "I promise there will be no drama."

I prayed like hell that, that was a promise I could keep. I wasn't sure how I'd respond if Cassim shot me down.

*

I parked in Sinn's driveway behind Cassim's car and checked the mirror before getting out. Before I got here, I stopped at Starbucks for two breakfast sandwiches and a Grande Caramel Macchiato. I didn't want to look like I was dying of starvation and like I was exhausted. I wanted Cassim to see me at my absolute best. I had to be on my A-game if I wanted to win this nigga back.

So, I got dressed in some skinny jeans which were slit at the knees, that looked painted on. They accentuated my shape perfectly. I wore an off the shoulder, crop top, and some cute strappy sandals. I made sure I beat my face, and I threw on one of my frontal wigs, and had it bone straight.

I flipped the sun visor back up and took a deep breath before getting out of the car. Barbecue smoke was coming from the backyard, so I went back there instead of knocking on the front door. I could see Nate playing in the pool on a floaty. DJ Khaled's I'm The One played at a low volume from speakers that are usually blasting.

Quavo!
I'm the one that hit that same spot
She the one that bring them rain drops
We go back, remember crisscross and hopscotch

You the one that hold me down when the block's hot
I make your dreams come true when you wake up
And your look's just the same without no make-up
Had to pull up on your mama, see what you're made of
Ain't gotta worry 'bout 'em commas 'cause my cake up

"Hey y'all," I said to Sinn and Luck who were standing at the grill with their backs to me.

Luck looked over his shoulder, sent me a quick head nod, and hurried into the house. Sinn shook her head and wiped her hands on the front of her apron, "Hey girl. I didn't tell them you were coming. He's probably going to wake that nigga up."

I stepped onto the deck, fumbling with my keychain, "Can I go inside?"

Sinn lightly chewed on her bottom lip and then said, "Yeah, go ahead. But listen... Symphony spent the night last night and—"

"And what," I snapped with raised eyebrows.

"Nothing happened... I'm just telling you so that you won't be alarmed when you see her. I know how crazy you are about that nigga and I don't want you clowning in front of my son, aight?"

I walked off and stormed into the house. Symphony sat at the island sipping from a cup of coffee. When I walked in, she looked over her shoulder at me with a snort and a dry good morning. I didn't say anything in return, I headed straight for the basement.

"He just woke up. He had a long night," said Symphony sitting there with a smirk, with both hands wrapped around the coffee mug she sipped from.

I snorted as my eyes averted from her to the pot of coffee siting on the coffee maker. I was about five seconds away from grabbing it and tossing what was left of it in her face.

I wondered, for a spit second, if Cassim had fucked this bitch. Sinn said that he was drunk as hell. Anything could have happened. I could take her being engaged in consideration, but she didn't give a damn about Todd. She was almost as stiff as plywood with him. She seemed like one of those bitches that were only in it for the money. And if that was the case, she wouldn't give a fuck about fucking my dude. Yes, my dude. That break up was one sided. I just been giving him some time to come to his senses. I've had enough now though.

Before I could get down the stairs, he was already climbing them, fixing his disheveled, ponytailed dreads.

"Good morning," I said to him.

He looked up at me and kept walking up the stairs. Despite the fact that I was standing there. Despite the fact that I was clearly unmoving. He walked up those stairs like he was going to walk straight through my ass if I didn't move. So, I stood my ass right there. He stood at the step right below the top one and said, "Excuse me, darling."

Symphony giggled. The bitch literally giggled. She knew that when Cassim used the word darling, it was not in a form of flattery.

I narrowed my eyes at him, "Don't call me that shit."

He grabbed my arms and moved me aside.

"Yo, Luck. You saw my car keys?" he said as he felt around his pockets for keys.

"I have them. You were trying to leave last night," said Symphony hopping down from the Bristol stool.

I stood there baffled like... why is this bitch trying me? Why are these mothafuckas trying me? I told Sinn I would be cool for the sake of Nate, and I will. I will kindly drag this bitch upstairs and beat her ass up there. He won't see it. I promise he won't know.

Symphony handed Cassim the keys, and he said, "Good lookin'."

"You know I got you," she said as she switched back over to her chair.

I chuckled and licked my lips, "Keep trying me... Keep fuckin' trying me."

Cassim paid me no attention as he moved around the kitchen to where the refrigerator sat. He opened it and grabbed some orange juice from it.

I sucked my teeth and walked over to him, "You really gone stand there like you don't see me?"

He sipped from the personal sized bottle of orange juice then asked, "What's good *killa*?"

That stung. I knew that was a jab at the abortion I had. He had a smirk on his face, and that bitch... that bitch was steady giggling.

I looked over my shoulder at her, "Bitch you better get the fuck up outta here with that cute shit before I jump over that island and beat the life out of you."

"This is my sister's house. I am welcomed—"

"Symphony," said Luck, coming up the basement stairs. "Chill yo. You know Nate out back. Go out there. Help Sinn on the grill."

"What?" she said like she was offended.

Luck just stood there staring at her. She turned the mug up to her mouth and hopped down from the Bristol chair. As she walked through the sliding doors that led to the deck, she mumbled some things under her breath.

"Cassim... can we talk?" I asked, standing there, steady fumbling with the big puff ball on my keychain.

Cassim eyes met mine, and a cool chill ran down my spine. The love… where was it? He moved around me, tossed the empty juice bottle into the trashcan, and told Luck to walk with him.

I felt alone. In a world populated by over seventy-five billion people; I felt alone.

He wasn't going to talk to me. He barely acknowledged my presence. He didn't care about me. The love I'd usually see in his eye contact. That look of 'finding it' was no longer there. Cassim didn't care about me anymore. How? How was it so easy for him to shut feelings out for me? Because I had an abortion? I mean, come on now, anybody with sense would have aborted that child.

I stood there in the kitchen unsure of what to do with myself. I had never felt so helpless in my life. I had never felt so lost either. Falling in love with that nigga had been a gift and a curse.

Sinn walked into the kitchen, and I got myself together. I scratched my head and thanked her for calling me about Cassim, but not to do it again.

On my way out of the house, he called my name. My heart skipped a beat, and butterflies filled the pit of my stomach. I quickly turned around with a smile, "Yeah?"

"Tell that nigga Juice to answer his fuckin' phone," he spat with a scowl on his face.

Shattered. My heart, it shattered into a billion pieces. I just nodded and walked out of the house.

When I made the decision to have the abortion, I never factored in how Cassim would feel if he found out. I kind of just brushed it under the rug, thinking that he never would. He found out, and I told him why it happened thinking that, that would change his perspective about things. But it hadn't. And most likely, it wouldn't.

"Ryann," said Sinn, jogging up behind me just as I had hit the unlock button on my keychain.

I looked over my shoulder at her, "Yeah?"

"Hold up," she leaned against my car, breathing heavy, tired as hell. "Good lawd, I'd like to faint. Anyway girl," she fanned herself. "Pretend you don't care. You show him that you care too much. Go find you a new nigga, I bet bread he gets his mind right. His mind ain't ever been right. But when he was with you.. he was different. Still… all you gotta do is crawl up under some new dick I bet—"

"I'm straight," I said cutting her off. "I'll be good."

It was a lie. And she knew it was a lie. She'd witnessed me at one of the most vulnerable stages in my life. I almost lost every bit of sanity I had when he was locked up for the short period of time. She knew just like everyone else in my life knew, that this break up—yeah, I can call it that now—was really taking a toll on me.

She placed her hand on my shoulder, "I ain't gotta worry about you pulling a Hannah Baker on me now do I?"

I chuckled and shook my head, "No, girl, I'm not good now, but I will be."

I glanced up at the house, at the sound of the door opening, and Cassim was coming out with Luck in tow. He looked over at me and then quickly looked away. Luck did the same thing. I noticed a glimmer of pity in his gaze though. I hated this. I hated that everybody knew about this breakup. I especially hated that Symphony knew. She had been standing by the gate watching Sinn and I talk the whole time. Straight goofy bitch that had been saved by the promise I made to Sinn about not beating her ass in front of Nate.

"Please call me if you need to talk. Listen, I know we met through that crazy nigga, but our friendship don't have to end because y'all relationship did," She waved me off. "He'll be back though. Just let him cool off. His ass is too into you to leave you alone. Trust me. I've been friends with Cass long enough to know that he wife's none! He did that with you. That means you're special."

I smiled a little, "Or, I was special." I sighed and said, "Alright Sinn. Take care."

"Me? Bitch.. you take care. You too fine—"

"Bye Sinn," I said with a laugh as I got into the car.

I stared up at him through the tints of my windows. He wore his dark tinted Buffs, but I knew that he was staring back at me too. I could feel it. Like I said before, his eye contact was so strong, that it was like he had lasers shooting from his pupils. And although, I couldn't see those black pearls called irises, I knew he was looking at me.

*

I couldn't just give up.

I needed him alone. So, I followed behind him. I kept my distance so that he wouldn't know I was creeping though. In the direction we were going, I knew that we were heading to the house. I didn't need to be on his tail to get to that place.

I know. I must look pretty fuckin' pitiful right now, but this love I share with Cassim… it's not one to just give up on. I'm fighting for this shit. And I'm going to force him to talk to me. I'm going to force him to touch me. If I could get him to do that, I'd win off rip.

As I was riding behind him, two police cars sped in front of me and hit their sirens, pulling him over. My heart rate sped up and I pressed my foot down on the gas pedal. What the fuck was going on, now? Why were they always bothering him? Cassim wasn't speeding. He was driving, minding his own business. What the hell was this about? I swallowed as I gripped the steering wheel, slowing up at the scene.

He'd stopped, and five cops approached his car with their guns drawn. I stopped and snatched my seatbelt off. I got out of the car, getting ready to approach him. We were just getting ready to get on the freeway and were driving on the service drive. There were cars riding behind me, but I didn't care. I didn't care about walking the streets of a busy road. I didn't like how they were pulling him over. With guns out, aggressively telling him to step out of the vehicle and shit, like he was a criminal.

I mean, duh, he is a criminal, but he had done absolutely nothing wrong.

"Hands on the back of your head," yelled one of the cops when Cassim finally got out of the car.

He saw me.

Our eyes locked before he was forced against the car.

"What is this about—

"You're under arrest for the murder of James, Sandra, and Shondra McGee...."

Everything after that was like a blur. This was not like before—when he was wanted down at the station for questioning. Oh no... they said he was under arrest... for the murder. A murder I knew he didn't commit. Why were they placing him under arrest for this? What happened?

I slammed my car door and ran towards them, "What—No! Let him go! He didn't do anything. He—he didn't kill them! Cassim—"

Crash!

Before I knew it, the wind had been knocked out of me and I was thrown up into the air. I didn't realize what had happened until I went crashing down onto the roof of a car I never saw coming.

Chapter 1 – Cass

"Nooooooo," I yelled, as I tried to fight the cops off me as I watched Ryann fall from midair on top of a car.

Ryann. Fucking Ryann.

"Stop resisting," yelled one of the cops with a gun pointed at me.

Before I knew it, I was being pushed to the pavement. A few feet away from me lied Ryann, on top of a car motionless.

"Get her some fuckin helped—"

Electricity shot through me and my body went into convulsions. Right after that, a gang of cops started to pound on me. For what? I'd already been fuckin' tazed. Through it all, all I cared about was Ryann, steady laid out on top of that car, twisted like a fucking pretzel.

Seconds later, the person who'd hit her, threw the car in reverse, resulting in Ryann sliding off the hood, crashing onto the pavement, and scurred off. I'd like to fucking lose it.

The officers surrounded me, blocking my view, but every now and then, I'd get a glimpse of her, and my soul would be set ablaze. I didn't care about the possibility of dying. I needed to touch her. I needed to make sure she was straight. But I couldn't move. I couldn't fuckin' move.

"Get him in the car, now!"

I was dragged to the police car, steady trying to fight them off. Shorty... she wasn't moving. She just lied there, twisted the fuck up, leaking. While everybody in traffic stood around recording.

I was fuming. I wanted to murk every last one of them standing around doing nothing.

"Is she dead? Oh my God, she looks dead," I heard somebody in the crowd say before I was literally thrown inside of the car.

*

"How is she?" I asked Luck with gritted teeth, as I gripped the handle of the phone with intensity.

Luck sighed, "I don't think this is the right time to—"

"How in the fuck is she, Luck?" I yelled through the phone.

He sighed again before saying, "Shorty won't wake up."

"What chu meanin, bruh? She in a fuckin' coma?"

I felt like my heart had been ripped out of my chest when he told me yeah. Fucking Ryann. Ryann.... Fucking Ryann! As soon as I peeped her swerve over when the cops pulled me over, I knew she was going to hop out going bananas.

What I didn't expect was for her to be hit. I couldn't get the image of her lying there, motionless out of my head. The shit had been haunting me since it happened. I couldn't get to a phone quick enough. As soon as they closed those bars, I went straight for the payphone.

I was silent for a minute, so Luck called out to me.

"Fuck," I breathed out.

"Listen bruh, keep yo shit together. Shorty's a rider—she'll pull through—"

"Shut the fuck up nigga, you don't know that shit. Don't come at me with nothing, but facts when it comes to Ryann, aight?"

I was snappy. These emotions... the feelings I felt behind possibly losing Ryann... they were foreign to me. I didn't like for things to be out of my control. I was held up in a jail cell for a crime I didn't commit, meanwhile... my fuckin' heart... she was laid up in the hospital in a coma. I felt hopeless. I didn't like to feel hopeless. I hadn't felt hopeless since I was a child.

This is why I never wanted to fall in love. I enjoyed not giving a fuck. Now, not giving a fuck was hard. When it came to her anyway.

"Aight, dawg. Look, keep a cool head in that bitch. Keep me laced."

"Aight, keep the boat afloat too nigga. I don't want to hear shit about it sinking in my absence. You hear me?"

"Bruh, I hear you."

I licked my lips, "Find out what the streets talm'bout. That one lil' bird bitch... see what she on."

Tiny was talking real greasy a few weeks ago, about how I needed to off myself for the shit I did. I had a gut feeling that shorty was behind me being in bars. I needed Luck to put his ear to the streets. I needed to know what them lil' young gossiping niggas was rapping about. I knew somebody was talking. Aside from the talking mafuckas were doing, I needed Scotty to get his ass here asap. I needed to know what them papers was looking like. It was a must that I knew for sure who had told lies on me.

"Bet it up, famo," said Luck before we ended our call.

I slammed the phone onto the hook and rested against the dingy grey walls of the cell I was held up in. I needed to get out of this bitch like pronto.

Being in confinement reminded me too much of my childhood. I stayed the fuck away from jail because this type of shit put me in a crazy headspace. All I saw was red as I stared at the nothingness of it all. I would lose my mind for sure if I didn't get out of here soon.

*

"Get me the fuck outta here, Scotty. I don't want to hear shit about any technical difficulties. None of that ol' bullshit, my nigga."

Did the fact that Scotty was white and I had called him a nigga mean anything to me? Shit no. I didn't associate the word nigga by color—I associated that shit by character. And right now, my man's Scotty was being ignorant, like those long years of law school taught him nothing.

Scotty leaned forward and said, "Don't you know I want to get you the fuck out of here bro? These mothafuckas have a serious hard on for you. And somebody talked. Somebody said they saw you leaving the McGee's house. That's bad for business. Bad for us!"

I waved him off and sat back in my chair with my arms folded over my chest, "Fuck outta here, Scotty. That murder was sloppy. Have you ever known me for being sloppy? With any of my shit? That shit that was done to those people? Fuckin' sick, my mans."

Scotty ran his hand over his blonde hair with a sigh, "What matters is motive and the fact that someone named you. Listen to me though. That shit won't stick. With no murder weapon and a solid alibi, I can get you out of here. I just need you cool and patient."

I laughed, "Well, what the fuck are we sitting here rapping for? Get. Me. The. Fuck. Outta here, cuz."

I was pissed. I was a ticking time bomb. I was annoyed. I was no good at this point. At this point, I was liable to smack the fuck out of a nigga. At this point, I was liable to do some shit that would really land me in this bitch. I was liable to crack a niggas head wide open for looking at me wrong. At this point, the niggas rocking badges meant nothing to me. In this mood, I would definitely get pig blood on me, and my nigga, I would do it with a grin on my face. At this point, it was fuck life. But hasn't it always been that way?

"It takes time, Cassim. Relax. Chill. You will be out—"

"Wanna switch spots, Scot? You wanna see how it feels to be locked up for a crime you didn't commit? Then you tell me if you'd be able to relax. Tell me if you'd be able to chill," I said through gritted teeth.

I had shit to do. I had moves to make. And I'm not talking about no drug shit neither. It was ready for me to put the group home in motion. You know how many fuckin' orphans out here going unfed? Going without proper healthcare? I needed shit to move. What was going to move with me sitting inside of a nasty ass jail cell? Not much. Shit was going to be on slow motion. I hated slow motion.

More important than any of that, I needed to make sure Ryann was straight. I needed to see her face. I needed to feel her skin up against mine. I needed to see the rise and fall of her chest. Not with the help of no fuck ass ventilator either. I wanted to grab her hand and for her to grab onto mine. I needed to make sure shorty still had life in her. A fucking coma?

Man nah, I needed shorty out here. I might've been a straight ass to her, but I loved her. I loved her more than I cared to admit and right now, I was full of regret. I should have been nicer. I should have showed her I cared. Fuck would it look like? Her leaving me out here after loving me the way she did? I would dead ass be lost out here.

Scotty sighed and sat back in his seat, "Alright man."

"Find out who put me in here too, my nigga. I need to know, like yesterday famo," I said with my eyes narrowed in on him.

He got up and nodded, "Alright. Let me work."

Chapter 2 – Ryann

Beep.
Beep.
Beep.
Beep.

I opened my eyes and had absolutely no idea as to where I was. I frantically looked around the room, in search of anything familiar, but nothing stood out. Not even the light skin girl who rushed over to my bed with a smile on her face.

"Oh, thank God you're awake, Ryann," she said as she reached out to grab my hand.

I flinched away, "Who the fuck are you? And where am I?"

Her eyebrows snapped together, and worry filled her face, "It's me... Omniel. You were in a horrible accident, Ryann. You don't know who I am?"

"No... I don't know you. Who... who is Ryann," I yelled, as my eyes averted from the IV lines dangling from my arm, to the cast covering my propped up leg. "Get away from me."

Tears cascaded down her cheeks as she slowly backed out of the room. I was in a horrible accident? Who was I? What accident? Who was she? I started to panic. I snatched the tubes from my nose, and the IV from my arm. Just as I was about to attempt to get out of bed a team of people in white coats walked into the room. I knew that they were doctors. I even knew that I was in the hospital. But I didn't have the common knowledge of people, names, or anything about myself.

"Good morning, Ms. Mosley," said one of the female doctors approaching me with a slight grin on her face. "My name is Doctor Sydney and I've been taking care of you since you came into my emergency room three days ago."

Three days ago, I thought to myself as my eyes frantically scanned the room for a way out.

"Please, Ms. Mosley, calm down and let me speak to you," said Dr. Sydney before asking everyone else to leave the room.

She then grabbed my hand and looked me in the eyes, "You were in a terrible hit and run accident. You were crossing the street and a vehicle struck you. As a result of severe head trauma, you are currently suffering from something called retrograde amnesia. Retrograde amnesia is a condition in which you lose memory of things that happened before the accident. Which is why you don't recognize your best friend, Omniel."

I sat there with my chest heaving and tears streaming down my face. All I wanted to do was leave. I felt like I was being lied to and that they had ulterior motives. I couldn't understand why what was happening, was happening.

"But," I swallowed, then whispered. "I don't know who I am."

She ran her soft hand over my bruised and scarred up arm, "It will all come back to you with proper treatment, Ryann. The amnesia is not permanent. What I need from you, dear, is for you to relax. It might sound strange, being that you've been in a coma for three days, but sweetie, I really need you to calm down."

She was slickly hooking my IV back up. I was too consumed with the thoughts roaming through my mind to protest. I needed answers.

"Is there anything you can remember?" she asked after taping my arm back up and putting the tubes back in my nose.

I sat there, thinking - or trying to at least. But nothing came up. I didn't know who my parents were. I didn't know how old I was. I didn't know my birthdate... which was fucking ironic because I had knowledge of those things, but I didn't know any of it about myself. How is it that, I knew I was supposed to have a name, and that I was supposed to have a birthdate, and that I was supposed to have family, but I didn't have the answers to the questions floating around my mind?

"No," I replied. "What do you know about me?"

She smiled and said, "Well, I know that your family's been by your side the whole time. You have three brothers who worship the ground you walk on. Chance, Justice and Adrien. Omniel, your best friend, you two met in elementary school and she's been here every single day. You have two other cousins too, who visit from time to time—

"What about my parents," I asked, noticing that she hadn't said anything about my parents.

She pulled her lips into her mouth before saying, "How about we get you something to eat and drink, then we'll talk later, okay?"

I didn't say anything. Instead, I lied there looking off into space. How was I supposed to get better if I didn't know how to? What was I going to do to refresh my memory? The bigger question in all of this was; Who am I? In addition to that question, I wondered... was I in love? How was my relationship with these brothers Dr. Sydney claimed I had? What had I done to deserve to be hit and just drove off on? That scared me. That question alone made me question who I really was?

Knock. Knock. Knock.

The girl from earlier, who Dr. Sydney called Omniel, peeked her head inside of the room and asked if it was okay for her to come in. Dr. Sydney looked down at me with questioning eyes and I just shrugged.

I didn't give a fuck. If this girl was truly my best friend, she had to know things about me. I was desperate at this point. Dr. Sydney wanted me to rest, but all I wanted to do was to get my memory back.

Five minutes later, Dr. Sydney left the room after telling me that she would have a food tray and water brought in immediately.

Omniel stood next to my bedside and reached out for my hand, which I did not give to her.

"You really don't remember me, Ryann?"

"No. I don't," I replied with an attitude. "I don't... I don't even remember myself."

Omniel gasped and I watched as a tear fell from her eyes, "Oh, Ryann."

Pity. She had pity in her eyes and I didn't like that. I didn't want pity right now. I wanted help.

"Gone on with that sad shit, alright? If you're not here to do anything but cry, you can just go. I'm the one that's hurt, what do you have to cry about?"

She giggled a little, "Damn girl, you sure you don't remember who you are? Ms. Ryann Marie Mosley is all up and through you, honey."

I didn't say anything. I hated this.

"Do you have a mirror," I asked.

The smile on her tear stained face faded away and she shook her head, "No. But... But I do have a hell of a lot of pictures of us. Of your brothers, and everything."

"I want to see my face. You have a camera on that phone. I want to see what I look like right now. I need to see what the accident did to me," I snapped.

She wanted to pacify me. But I didn't need pacifying. I needed this Omniel bitch to leave. I needed someone here who was going to give me the real, regardless of what it might do to me.

"I just don't think that's—

"Bye. Go. Please go," I said as I lifted my arm to point at the door.

Just as I did, there was two soft knocks, and shortly after someone walked in carrying a food tray and a cup of water.

"Hey girl. I'm so happy you finally woke up," she said as she sat the tray and water on the table next to my bed. She flashed me her I.D badge and smiled, "I'm Alisha. I've been your patient care assistant since you got here. Anyway, yes girl... I've been waiting for you. You are surely a walking testimony, okay? Not only did you survive that tragic hit and run, but honey... your baby did too. Amen!"

My eyes damn near popped out of socket, "What?!"

"Ryann, boo, lie back," said Omni, giving the nurses aide a nasty glare. "What the fuck is wrong with you?"

Alisha drew back, "What? Wait... she didn't know?"

"No, she did not! Y'all need to get the communication in order around this bitch! Ryann has amnesia and you just—

I pushed Omni away from me and tried to get out of the bed. But, didn't get too far because of my broken leg. I was distraught and furious at this point. This lady just told me I had a baby. A fucking baby? Where is it? Was it okay? What condition was he or she in? I have a baby? Then where in the fuck is the daddy?

Crash!

As soon as I got out of the bed, I went crashing down onto the hardwood floors. Seconds later, the room was full of unfamiliar faces and I felt like I was being attacked. The biggest, burliest of the three men who entered the room, effortlessly picked me up from the floor and delicately placed me back in bed. When I tried to get up again, he held me down by my wrist.

"Where is my baaaaaaby? Get off of me! Get off," I screamed and cried.

Sadness filled his eyes as he looked into my eyes with a quivering bottom lip, "I'm sorry, Ry baby. I'm so sorry."

I kicked my uninjured leg and squirmed around the bed as much as I could, trying to get free. I didn't know these people. Everyone was just surrounding my bed, looking down at me with wrinkled eyebrows and pity.

"Everybody out please," yelled Dr. Sydney, the only one I trusted.

She stood next to my bed, rubbed the big guy's arm and told him that she would take it from there. He looked at her with a scowl so deep, that Dr. Sydney took a step back with her hands up.

"Goose," yelled the light skin one with curly hair. "Let the lady do her job."

"But—

"Come on, G," said the other guy, shaking his head with misty eyes.

*

Fifteen minutes later, Dr. Sydney had calmed me down. She sat on side of my bed humming a melody I didn't know while comforting me by rubbing my hand. She was the only one I let touch me. She was the only one I was going to let touch me.

"My baby. Where is my baby," I asked, with tears rolling down the sides of my face.

Dr. Sydney sighed and pointed at my belly, "Right there, Ryann. Growing inside of you. She feels whatever it is that you feel. That is why I need you to stay calm. I need you to relax."

"She? I'm having a girl," I asked as my hands immediately went over my stomach.

Dr. Sydney chuckled a bit, "No, dear. It's too early to tell. I'd just rather say she than it."

I didn't say anything. I lied there with my hands rubbing back and forth on my flat belly, thinking. Or trying to think at least. I searched my mind for answers. I tried my hardest, but I came up with nothing.

"When will my memory return?"

"It varies, Ryann. But I will have your family and friends bring some pictures up for you to look at. For now though, I'd rather you just rest. Today was very stressful. I'm going to tell your family to come back tomorrow, okay? You've gone through a lot today."

I nodded in agreement. It wasn't like I knew those people anyway.

*

The next morning, I woke up to the sound of my own voice. Sitting next to my bed were the three men Dr. Sydney said were my brothers. I looked up at the television screen with furrowed eyebrows. I was smiling and joking around with the big one, while the light skin one sat on the couch smoking a cigarette looking down at his phone. Until I walked over and snatched it out of his hands. I was yelling at him about being on his phone 'knowing I missed them'. Apparently they hadn't come by for a few days.

The other one with the individual braids must've been recording because I heard him, but didn't see him.

"Good morning, Ry," said the big one with a huge grin on his face. "Do you remember us now?"

Something was wrong with him. He was the biggest of the three, but his behavior was one of a child. I glanced away from him, back up to the TV screen and in the video, he wasn't like this. In the video, he seemed... normal.

"It don't work like that, G. Let her watch," said the light skin one with a frown on his face and his arms crossed over his chest. He always looked so mean, like he didn't want to be bothered. Well, if he didn't want to be bothered, he could get the fuck on.

"Why are you here if you don't want to be? Trust, you will not be missed. I don't even know your ass," I snapped.

The young one with the braids laughed and approached the bed, "We're here because we love yo mean ass, Ryann."

"Exactly," said the mean one. "You think we would have that video playing if we didn't care?"

"Stop being mean to her," said the big one with his fists balled.

The young one looked down at his fist and snorted, "Be easy, bruh."

"Where are my parents?" I asked.

The room fell silent, until Dr. Sydney and her team came in.

The mean one stood up and approached them, approaching my bed, "Yo, how long is she going to be like this and shit? Ain't y'all supposed to be fixing her?"

Why was it that every time I asked about my parents, people ignored me? Were they hurt in the hit and run too? Did they die or something? The shit was bugging me. I couldn't understand why they weren't in any of the videos that were playing. They weren't in the pictures in the slideshow that played after the video stopped neither.

"These things take time, Justice," said Dr. Sydney to the mean one. "We've gone over this already."

"How much time," asked Justice.

"Where are my parents," I yelled.

Justice looked over his shoulder at me, and then back at Dr. Sydney who nervously licked her lips.

"Stop avoiding the fucking question. I'm their daughter, right? They're supposed to be here," I yelled, before punching the bed.

The one with the braids roughly ran his hands over his braids, "Look, Ryann. They busy and all that. Out of town and shit, on business."

The big one narrowed his eyes at him and folded his arms over his big chest, "What—

Justice interrupted him by pushing him away from the bed, "Just get better, aight, sis?" he paused and kissed me on the cheek. "Just worry about that. We love you—me," he pointed at himself, "Juice. Goose," he pointed at the big one, "and Adrien." He concluded by pointing at the one with braids. "Find us in that big ass head of yours, aight?"

I chuckled a little. Because for the first time since I've seen him, he was nice. He treated me like he actually cared about me. The other two, Goose, and Adrien, stood at my bed.

Goose held his hands out and said, "Dr. Sydney, I'm gon' have to ask you and yo peoples to leave, ma'am."

Dr. Sydney looked over at me, to make sure I was cool, I guess. And I gave her a reassuring smile. She nodded and told me that they would be back later.

Once the door was closed, Goose grabbed hold of one of my hands. When Juice didn't bulge to grab the other he yelled his name with gritted teeth. Adrien nudged Juice in the side, and he reluctantly grabbed hold of my other hand.

"Bow y'all heads," commanded Goose.

We did. And he started to pray.

"Dear father God, we ask you Lord, to heal our sister. Do yo work and shit, fix her. So she can fix me," he said like a damn maniac. "I need Ry, and she needs us. So, fix her. Fix her so she can fix me."

"Yo, what the fuck is this nigga talm'bout," mumbled Adrien.

I snickered and Goose snapped telling us to respect the Lord. How? When he'd just blatantly cursed while speaking to the Lord he wanted us to respect. I didn't know them too well, but I could tell off top that Goose was clearly missing a few marbles.

Chapter 3 - Cass

"Find out who it was, Scott."

"None of this matter though, Cassim," said Scotty, inching in closer to me. "Your alibi is rock solid. They have to let you go on those grounds alone. Listen to me man, I'm trying to keep everything cool."

I sat back in my chair and crossed my arms over my chest, with my head slightly cocked back. All of what Scotty was saying to me sounded good. My alibi checked out, as I knew it would because I didn't do shit. I was at the crib, and the gate man was the one to vouch for that, along with the surveillance of me pulling in and never leaving. But right now, all I could think about was finding out who ratted on me. It had to be that thot ass bitch Tiny. Who else could it have been? Bitch had it out for me on the serious tip. If there was anybody in the hood who had ratted, it was that bird bitch.

Scotty wanted me cool. He wanted to keep that piece of information away from me because he didn't want me out here on animal shit.

"You're out of here, Cassim. Did you hear me?" asked Scotty. "As soon as we get out of here, we can get the ball rolling on the center. Remember?"

He brought up the group home as a reminder of why I needed to stay cool. I didn't need a reminder. I knew what I stood to lose. Knowing that, I still wanted the mothafuckas blood on me. Period.

I didn't say anything. I sat there rubbing my beard with twisted lips. Although I had my speculation, I was a man who needed facts. I needed to know for a fact that shorty had ran her lips. Especially since the bitch was carrying. It'd kill me if I sent niggas to do her in, and she ended up being innocent.

Scotty looked from side to side and whispered, "Look man, cool out."

I gave him a half smile, "I am cool."

I was cool. I didn't have any other choice but to be—for now at least.

Scotty stood up and grabbed the handle to his briefcase, "Twenty minutes tops, Cassim. Keep your head down and don't do anything to piss these fuckers off."

I pinched the bridge of my nose with a head nod and stood up, "Twenty minutes Scotty. Twenty minutes is all you've got."

Seconds later, the CO came back into the room, cuffed me, and escorted me back to my cell.

*

Twenty minutes later, I was out just as Scotty promised. Them pigs didn't want to let me go. I walked by them pussieswith a grin on my face. Ho niggas had a serious hard on for a nigga they could not touch. Shit dead ass pissed them off.

As soon as I stepped outside, I slapped hands with Luck who was leaned up against my whip.

"What's the deal, fam?" I said as I moved around to the other side of the car to hop in.

"Niggas talkin' crazy, hop in. Let's rap," he said as he opened the passenger door.

I saluted Scotty as he got into his car and he saluted me back. Bro always looked out. No matter how serious the case or the charge, he got me off. Straight official with his shit, regardless of the mess I gave him. If there is anybody who understands when I'm on tip, it's him. He's been dealing with me since we were young niggas with dreams and ambitions.

"What's good, G?" I asked as I pulled out of the parking lot. "What it's looking like, fam?"

He pulled a blunt from behind his ear and sparked fire too it while shaking his head, "Ali. Niggas thought it was a rap fa sho, fam. Boy was about ready to cut all ties."

"Pussy ass Mexican really thought I was going to rat, huh?" I said as I ran my hand over my beard.

I wasn't surprised to hear about my connect, Alejandro, talking about cutting ties. It business. But niggas know me, and that talking shit ain't never been my forte.

Luck pulled from the blunt, "Shit chea. Cat want a sit down. He wanna see where shit at with that case."

"Set it up. We can fly out there first thing in the morning."

Business is always top priority, but right now what mattered more than anything was going to see Ryann. I needed to make sure she was straight. If she was straight, then I was straight. It was later for that Ali shit. That nigga could dead ass wait. Fuck em. Serves him right for mistaking me for a stupid ass fuck nigga.

"Them cats already on US soil," said Luck with raised eyebrows. "As soon as they got word that you was in that joint, they hopped on a jet. That nigga Ali stay on it with his scary ass. Dawg hit my line about your release right after Scotty called me to scoop you. They want to link tonight."

I smirked as I took a pull from the blunt before passing it back to Luck. Of course, Ali was already here. Me having trouble with the law was not only bad business for me—it was bad business for everyone connected. I stayed out of trouble just to avoid sit downs with Ali. I couldn't stand the fat fuck.

"Where they posted up at?" I asked, slightly choked up on weed smoke.

"You already know how that nigga roll. Secret location," said Luck with a smirk.

I smirked back and asked him where Ali was posted up at again.

Luck laughed and told me exactly where Ali was. If there was a nigga who could find a mafucka it was him. It was Luck who got me the location of that ho ass Uber driver.

"I'll link with that nigga after I make sure shorty smooth."

I didn't give a fuck about meeting with Ali. I had to make sure shorty was straight. The fear of losing her really had me shook out here. I've never gave a fuck about anybody—myself included. Giving a fuck about people serves as a weakness. I didn't need a weakness. Not in this game.

"You sure you want this nigga waiting? You know he know you out," said Luck before inhaling a thick cloud of smoke.

"Fuck I look like caring? That nigga can wait."

Luck nodded with his lips turned down, "Yo call nigga."

It was always my call. Luck was my right-hand man, but at the end of the day, I made the decisions. And if I wanted Ali to wait, he would wait. Fuck that nigga gone do? Come snatch me up? Dawg can try. If he know I'm out, then he know that case was flaw. Fuck 'em.

"Always my call, brodie. Now pass me that good green, hoggin' ass fuck boi," I joked with a smirk.

Luck passed me the weed back and we chopped it up about the way shits been going with the cash flow. Nothing about that had changed. Bread had been at a steady flow and that was always music to my ears. One thing I can say about Luck is that he steps the fuck up whenever I'm away. That's why this nigga is my right-hand man. Couldn't have a better man for the job.

Chapter 4 – Ryann

"Ryann, are you sure you're up for this many visitors," asked Dr. Sydney looking around my crowded hospital room.

"If these people are my family like you say they are, then yes. I want them here. I think it'll help," I said with a slight smile.

I had been awake for a couple of days now and my memory was still fuzzy. I knew who I was now. I knew my full name, and my date of birth. I still didn't know who anyone was though. I met a doctor who specializes in amnesia yesterday and he gave me a few pointers, and has also been in touch with my family. It was Dr. Calhoun who suggested the video my brothers played for me the other day.

"Right, so gone on about yo business, lady," said Ashlee.

Dr. Sydney snickered and left the room.

I picked up a lot of shit about Ashlee. She ran her mouth a lot, and I just 'met' the bitch this morning. From what I've picked up about her, I could tell me and this bitch bumped heads a lot.

"Cass still ain't been up here," she asked with a snort.

"Who is Cass," I asked with furrowed eyebrows.

"Aw shit, you don't remember him either," she asked with an eye roll.

"LeeLee," said Juice with a scowl on his face. "Chill."

Ashlee twisted her lips up and rolled her eyes, "Shut up Juice. What? You worried about the mention of Cass gone snap her back to reality?"

I laid there paying attention to everything. Body language, tone of voice, and all of that. And those two mothafuckas... they were hiding something.

"Anyway, Cass—

"Stop LeeLee, you know Cass is locked up," said Shaneka, with wide eyes and her hands on her hips. "Well, shit for the sake of Tiny's life, I sure hope he still is."

I started to feel a bit overwhelmed. They kept talking about people outside of this room. I didn't like that because I was having a hard time remembering them as is, and they were making the shit even harder by mentioning different people.

"Do me a favor," I said, as I shifted around my bed to get comfortable. "Save the gossiping and shit for when y'all are outside of my room aight?"

"Right. She don't need this shit right now," said Omniel sitting right next to my bed like she did every time she visited me.

She had such a positive spirit about her. I've really grown to like Omniel. I could tell why we were best friends for so long.

I picked up the prenatal pill Dr. Sydney left me and tossed it down my throat. I could see Shaneka staring at me with a funny look on her face in my peripheral. Who are these bitches? I swear I got bad vibes from her and her sister. There was no way in hell that we could've been as close as I was told we were. Nah, these ho's gave me bad vibes all around.

"Nobody's trying to gossip," said LeeLee with a deep scowl, staring at Omniel. "Fuck you even here for? Bitch you ain't family."

"Yo," yelled Juice with a scowl. "Ashlee you gotta go."

Omniel rolled her eyes, "Yes, bitch, please go. Ryann don't need this shit right now. Damn, what is wrong with you?"

Ashlee snatched her purse up off the windowsill and stormed out of the room without saying good bye to me.

*

Shortly after Ashlee left, everyone else did too and I was relieved. I was tired of my room being crowded, especially today. Shit went left real fast. Drama was the last thing I needed. I needed peace at this stage of my recovery and the only one who seemed to actually give me that was Omniel. So as soon as they left, I had my nurse shut my drapes and close my door up.

A knock on my room door snatched my attention away from a gameshow playing on the TV. I grabbed the string dangling over my head to turn the light on.

"Come in," I answered.

It was three o'clock and I was due for my next set of vitals. I sat up, and reached over to grab my cup off the table.

"Y'all are like clockwork in here," I said before taking a sip of my water.

"Are they?"

The sound of a deep, baritone voice startled me and I dropped my cup on the floor. The water in it, splashed up into my face as I turned around to see who he was.

Our eyes met when he stepped further into my dimly lit room. Behind his dark eyes sat sadness, worry, and a tinge of anger. Behind mine sat uncertainty, and fear.

He approached my bed and reached out for my hand, "Ryann."

I moved away, with furrowed eyebrows as I stared into the eyes of a complete stranger. Or was he? The crinkle in his brow, and the tone of his voice, were heavily coated in passion. He was sad.

He ran his big hands down his dark face with a sigh, "You don't know me?"

"Should I?"

He crouched down next to my bed, and ran his calloused hands along my cheek. I let him. It was the way my body responded to his touches. The familiarity. The love. The tingles that shot through my body when he touched me... I knew this man. Perhaps I loved him? Was he the father of my child?

He brushed his thumb over my bottom lip, which was still a tad bit damp from the water I sipped from before I dropped it on the floor. I closed my eyes and let him touch me in provocative ways. I let him because... because my body wanted to let him. I couldn't push him away.

"Who are you," I whispered against his thumb.

"Cassim."

"What are..."

I lost my voice. What was happening to me? I wanted to know what we were to one another. I wanted to ask him why the rest of the rest of the world no longer matter to me. I wanted to ask him why the beat of my heart was so loud. I wanted to know why for just a second, time felt to move as slow as molasses. But my heart... the heavy beating of it... it was... it was so fast. It beat so hard that I could see every thump through the thin fabric of my hospital gown.

Cassim. He was doing this to me.

"Breathe." he said, his full lips rubbing against my earlobe.

How? How did I forget to breathe?

I opened my eyes, and a tear unintentionally fell from the one on the right.

"Why is this... what is this," I said, stammering over my words.

"Infatuation," said Cassim, now holding onto my hand.

He put it up to his chest, and placed it right on his heart.

"Do you remember me," he asked, with his cold, black eyes centered in on my tear drenched ones.

"No," I struggled to say. "My mind says no. But my heart says yes."

He let my hand go and walked away from the bed. I watched him walk out of the room defeated.

The door slammed shut, and finally, the rest of the world came alive. The laughter on the TV, and the steady humming of the air conditioning system filled my ears. My eyes averted over to the IV pump which had been beeping for the past hour... but when Cassim was here... I hadn't heard a thing.

My eyebrows snapped together, and I snatched my phone from the nightstand. Was it him? The mysterious man from my pictures? The guy who rarely focused on the camera? The one I took pictures of while he slept?

I zoomed in on one of the pictures in my phone and gasped. It was him. Maybe I would have recognized him before if it hadn't been for my room being so dim.

It was him.

The man Omniel said I was in love with. She described the love I had for him as potent. And it was. The way he made me feel just by a simple touch... it told me things. It told me that it was not my heart that said yes, but it was my soul.

"Cassim," I whispered.

As if he'd heard me call him, the door to my room opened and in he came... only this time he was carrying a camera.

He licked his lips and said, "One day I asked you why you took so many pictures of me... and you said," he paused and chewed on his bottom lip before saying, "You said for when you grow old and forget. I mean, shit, forgetting came a little sooner than you had hoped but... here, just look."

He handed me the camera, and began to scroll through the many pictures. There were hundreds. All of him. Standing on a balcony with his dreadlocks hanging over his shoulders. Sitting on the hood of a car. And there was this one... there was snow... and his dark skin against it was like a splash of black paint on white wall.

I swallowed, and shook my head with tears wetting my eyes. It was all too overwhelming. I couldn't remember him, and I wanted to. I wanted to so bad because, he seemed like someone to remember. The way my body responded to him... the way my heart beat against my chest... he was special to me. He had to be.

"Ryann," he called out.

I looked away from the pictures, and up into his eyes. He wore a frown on his face. I couldn't tell if it was because he was sad, mad, confused, or just frustrated.

"I don't...I can't remember," I replied with a shaky voice.

He grabbed the camera from me, nodded, and sat it on the side table, "It's aight, sweetheart."

He then stepped back, kicked his shoes off and told me to move over. I did, and seconds later, he was lying beside me with his face pressed against the side of my bruised and battered face. His prickly facial hair rubbed against my cheek, and his warm breath beat against my ear.

Cassim whispered, "It's okay. I'll wait for you."

I took a deep breath and melted into him. I rested against his face, resting up against the side of mine and closed my eyes. I could feel the steady beat of his heart beating against my arm. The beat of it calmed me down in ways I hadn't been calmed since I woke up here. I finally felt at peace.

True, I didn't know who he was. To me, he was a stranger, but to my body and soul, he was not.

Cassim rubbed my arm as he lied there, telling me everything about himself, how we met, and how he tried not to fall in love with me but failed miserably.

I learned all about his childhood, how he was neglected and sent to foster home after foster home. He told me how he found out about all of the pictures I had taken of him before we even met. He told me that I was infatuated with him before I even knew him. And because I loved him regardless of his flaws that made falling in love with me inevitable.

I absolutely loved lying in his arms listening to the deep, raspy sound of voice. I loved learning about a love that I had forgotten about. It was beautiful. It just pained me a little, knowing that I had forgotten something so amazing.

*

The next morning, I was awaken by the nurse assistant telling me it was time for my vitals. When I opened my eyes, it was like my mind had gone through a reboot and I was hit with a series of flashbacks. It was all so overwhelming. A ton of memories flashing through my mind, replaying like a movie being sped up on the fast forward setting.

Cassim sat up out of his sleep, and looked into my wandering eyes with furrowed eyebrows. He ran his big hand over the wrapping over my head, and told me everything was going to be alright.

And then it happened. Memories of us, played through my mind like a ghetto love story. The smiles. The tears. The sex. ***The passion***.

My eyes stopped wildly moving around, in search of focus, and locked in on his. He looked back at me, searching my eyes for the memories we shared. Searching my eyes for familiarity. And I gave it to him because I did remember.

"Ryann—

"I remember you," I said. "I remember everything."

He let out a sigh of relief and wrapped his strong arms around me, "I thought I lost you."

He was so full of emotion. This was a side of Cassim that was new to me. Although I remembered him, my memory was still a bit foggy but I knew for a fact that he had never shown this side of himself to me.

"Thank God," yelled the nurse assistant. "Hallelujah. Who are you? You her boyfriend? She share the news with you yet? This is a glorious day! Thank the Lord."

"Why don't you go find my doctor and tell her that I'm getting my memory back aight? I thought I told them I didn't want you as my nurse assistant anymore. What the fuck," I snapped.

Cassim was so wrapped up in me, that he hadn't heard anything my nurse assistant had said. He stared into my eyes with so much passion that it was almost as if he'd forgotten about the abortion. He stared at me like he wasn't mad at me before the accident. I wondered, if the news of my pregnancy would change anything. Would we be together? Low key, I didn't want that. I wanted Cassim to want me because of me. Not because I'm pregnant.

"Fuck," he said before closing his eyes and sighing.

I leaned into his hand resting on my cheek and asked, "What's wrong?"

"You scared the shit out of me Ryann Mosley. Don't ever fuck around and almost die on me again," He said as he slowly opened his eyes, moving his hand from my cheek to my lips.

I lightly chuckled, "Listen... I have to tell you something."

He grabbed my hands and kissed my fingertips, "Mmhmm?"

"I'm pregnant," I blurted out before chewing on my bottom lip.

He stopped kissing my fingertips, and his eyebrows shot up. He scratched the tip of his nose, and climbed out of the bed. I couldn't read him. I couldn't tell if he was happy or upset.

"Say something."

Cassim pulled the cover off my body and lifted my hospital gown. He then ran his big hands over the flatness of my belly. He crouched down and kissed it before lying his head on it.

He pressed his ear against my belly and said, "Don't take this one away from me."

I rolled my eyes, "Why would I do that? You know why I did that shit the last time—

"Good morning, Ms. Ryann," said Dr. Sydney walking into my room with a huge grin on her face.

Cassim stayed right where he was, with his ear pressed against my belly. Every so often, he'd kiss it, and go right back to listening to my belly.

"Good morning, Dr. Sydney," I said with a smile while Cassim rubbed my thighs.

Dr. Sydney giggled, "Dad? You're dad?"

Cassim stood up and nodded with his hands stuffed into his pockets.

Dr. Sydney reached into the pocket of her doctor coat and pulled something out, "This right here is a fetal Doppler. It's a device that picks up the sound of the babies heartbeat. Now, Ryann is fairly early, but we can search for one if you'd like."

"Definitely," said Cassim with a half-smile.

"But first, I need to speak with Ryann about her memory. I hear you're starting to remember?"

I nodded with a huge smile on my face, "Yes, Dr. Sydney. Some things are still slightly foggy, but I've gotta say, I remember quite a bit."

I did. The memory that stood out the most to me was what was going on between Cassim and I. Things were rocky, but yet he was here. He was worried. He still loved me, but that didn't cancel out what happened before. The way he's been playing me. It was all very clear.

"I'm still having some difficulty remembering far back, but I can recount some of what's happened within the past month," I continued.

"That's great progress, Ryann," she exclaimed. "You might be out of here sooner than I expected. We've gotta get you walking around more too." She stepped closer to my bed and pulled a tube of gel from her coat, "Now, let's check on this baby."

The entire time Dr. Sydney spoke to me, Cassim kept his eyes on mine. I was still kind of pissed about that comment he made about not taking the baby from him. What the fuck did he take me for? A monster? I had an abortion. Okay… I was raped too. What about that isn't he understanding?

After Dr. Sydney finished up, I rubbed my lips together and asked Cassim about him being pulled over. I remembered. I remembered everything that led up to my accident. And if I heard correctly, he was being arrested for murder.

"Didn't stick. My alibi was rock solid," he said flatly, running his hand back over my stomach.

"That's great. I'm happy you're here. And I hope that we can move past that one thing."

He didn't say anything. He stood there nodding, steady rubbing my stomach.

"Did you hear me," I called out.

"I heard you. Just let me enjoy this right here, alright?"

I nodded and closed my eyes, happy for the moment. Hoping and praying that this moment would last forever. Happiness between Cassim and I.

Chapter 5 – Cass

Pregnant?

Shorty's fucking pregnant. When she told me that, I was literally lost for words. I was ecstatic. I felt like, fuck, maybe this is God's way of telling me to chill out. Like here nigga, here goes another one. But I'd be lying if I said that the thought of possibly having two didn't cross my mind. I pushed it out of my head though, because the last thing I wanted to do was upset Ryann considering her condition.

Pregnant. Baby is pregnant and the baby is fine. Shit crazy. I stood there, watching the way Ryann was thrown into the air when she got hit. I saw how hard she fell onto the ground once the car sped off. I saw it all, and the shit was nasty. It amazes me how the baby is perfectly fine after all of that. Baby got that solider DNA running through 'eem. DNA of a straight G.

My phone rang and I pulled it from my pocket. I smirked at the sight of Ali's name.

"What's good, Ali," I casually answered like the fat fuck wasn't looking for me.

"How long before you're home, Cassim?" he said, sounding like he was choked up from cigar smoke.

"You at my residence, my mans?" I asked with gritted teeth just as I pulled up at the gate.

"You wouldn't come to me, so," he paused and coughed. "So, I came to you."

I hung up on him and drove up to the gate. The gatekeeper stood there with bucked eyes, as if he'd seen a ghost. Ali probably threatened to cut his balls off and shove 'em down his throat if he didn't let him in. I cut my eyes at him and he started to apologize profusely as I drove through the opened gates.

I could see Ali's black Rolls Royce casually parked in my drive way. He stood outside of the car, leaned on it, smoking on a cigar with both of his bodyguards on both sides of him. I pulled up in the driveway behind his car and quickly hopped out.

Ali approached me with an opened palm, and I looked down at it with my top lip curled up.

"Let's wrap this shit up," I said with a scowl. "And Mush? You can stay yo fat neck ass right where you standing. Hugo, you too. I don't need you niggas stepping in my crib. Straight disrespectful to come to a niggas home unannounced. Be grateful I didn't greet you clowns with bullets."

Ali chuckled, "Come on man. Keep it friendly."

"That's what I'm doing, G. Otherwise I would have really greeted you with slugs."

I kept walking, despite the fact that Hugo and Mush were standing there with their hands on the handle of their burners. Not an ounce of fuck was given.

Regardless of what came out of my mouth, Ali would never let 'em squeeze off on me. I was his top selling customer. Pissing a bitch about me being disrespectful wasn't going to do anything for his pockets.

I unlocked the door to my house, with Ali following behind me. I looked over my shoulder at him, "Do me a favor and put that stinking ass cigar out, fam."

He dropped it and stomped on it before following me into the house.

He looked around my little spot with his mouth turned down, "Nice."

"What's good Ali?" I asked before closing the door behind me.

He shrugged, "I'm trying to see what's going on with you, my friend."

"You know what's going on with me. Get to the point. I've got shit to take care of. You know I've been out of commission. You know the case is a done. No evidence. Solid alibi. You came out here for nothing. I don't talk, you know this."

I didn't like the back and forth. Never been a small talk type of cat. I wanted to get straight to the point, but this nigga Alejandro wanted to ease into the conversation. Fuck all 'lat.

"You sure?" he asked with raised eyebrows.

"Ali, you're a man of many connection. Dig deeper, aight? You really wasted your time coming all the way out here."

He shrugged, "I needed a vacation."

"No one vacays to Michigan. Fuck outta here, Ali."

"Why so angry?" he asked before running his tongue over his bottom lip.

"You find this lil' shit funny, uh?" I asked as I slowly approached him. "You pulled up at my crib to send a nonverbal message. But listen, I can give you that same message, Alejandro. No one is invincible. You bleed like I bleed. You can be touched just as much as I can be touched. The difference between you and I?" I shrugged. "I don't give a fuck. I don't ride around with bodyguards because shit like death… it fears me none. It terrifies you. Terrifies you so much that you move every year. Moving won't save you though, Ali. It won't."

Ali wasn't known for being ruthless. He was known for being a pussy with a lot of muscle. Period. He moved around so much because he was paranoid. If it wasn't for his grade A product, and the hundred or so soldiers he had on payroll, he would have been murked a long time ago. Mafuckas weren't intimated by Ali; they were intimated by his muscle. Me? I wasn't intimidated by any of it. I didn't bite my tongue when it came to this nigga and it irritated the fuck out of him.

Ali ran his hand over his wild, short hair with a chuckle, "Cass, Cass, Cass." He shook his finger at me, "You're lucky you make me a lot of money. Otherwise, it would have been off with your head a long time ago." He sighed, "I'm happy to hear that everything is peachy. I'll be in touch if necessary."

I walked away from him, heading to the shower, "I would say it's been a pleasure speaking with you, but we both know that would be a lie. Safe travels though, man."

*

"How much is it?" I asked Luck before pulling from the blunt.

Luck dropped the heavy duffle bag on the table in front of me and said, "Fifty thou."

I held the blunt in between my lips and scooted to the edge of the couch to open the duffy up. Unzipping it, I reached inside, enjoying the feel of fresh drug money on my hands. Shit. Fifty K that easy?

"What it look like? Squeaky," I asked Luck.

He nodded, "You know how them niggas move. Ali won't have a clue it was us behind the shit."

Alejandro disrespected me by coming to my residence. I disrespected him by having his 'secret location' hit two days later. Got the pussy nigga for fifty thousand, easy. Bitch nigga had violated, so I violated him.

Smooth lil' mission, quick lil come up off another nigga. I ain't never been into thievery, but then again, I ain't never been into being disrespected either. I could have easily had his life taken away from him but I still needed Ali. The drugs he supplied me with were top notch. Fuck would I get my shit from if I had his wig split?

"What's the word on that other thing," I asked as I dumped ashes from the blunt.

Luck looked up from the racks he was collecting for himself and said, "I got it in motion. It's takin a lil' longer, but it's moving, G."

I nodded and rested on the back of the couch.

Chapter 6 – Ryann

"You about ready to get out of here, ain't you?" said Shaneka, resting against the foot of my bed.

I was ready. Too damn ready. My memory had improved substantially since the first flashback, which was a week ago. These days, memories came with triggers. Seeing Shaneka for the first time this week brought up memories of our fight, and the way she'd been acting funny and shit. I finally knew why the vibe between us was weird. I beat her ass.

"I should be getting out of this bitch soon. The neurologist is coming to see me today. Hopefully he clears me to go home."

"Are you going home? Or over to Cass's house," she asked with a smirk.

"Nah. I'm going home. I don't know what's what between us and I honestly don't even want to force anything."

Cassim had been here every day since his first visit. He was the absolute sweetest. But I felt like he was only being nice because what happened scared him. Staring into his eyes, I saw the uncertainty. I could tell that he still wasn't quite over the abortion. An abortion we haven't even discussed. I steered clear of that topic because I had no desire to argue with him about it.

"He still not over the abortion, huh?" she sadly said.

I snatched my eyes away from the television and narrowed them at her. I didn't remember telling Shaneka about the abortion. At this point of my recovery, my memory was still a bit foggy. Maybe I did. So, instead of jumping the gun and going off, I went along with it. Drama did my memory no good.

"Girl, no. He's pissed about it," I said shaking my head.

Shaneka slowly treaded to the side of the bed, picked my hair brush up, and began to softly brush my hair, "It's alright. He'll come around." She shrugged, "And if he don't, then so be it. You can do a lot better than a drug dealing killer anyway."

I snatched away, "Yo, chill out bitch."

Cassim and I were still at odds, but I'd be damned if I sat back and let Nek's hood rat ass talk down on him. It'd be a cold day in hell before I let anybody disrespect that man.

She held her hands up, "I'm just sayin."

"Stop just sayin all of the time Shaneka. Sometimes your two cents are just not needed. Especially when it comes to me and my shit."

Shaneka pulled her lips into her mouth and nodded, "I get it. My bad. I overstepped boundaries."

Shaneka had been overstepping a lot of boundaries lately. I had been giving her the side eye for a while now. Something was off about her. She had gone from my favorite cousin, to a bitch I just didn't want to kick it with anymore.

"It's cool," I flatly said as I flicked through TV channels.

She let out an exasperated sigh, "Alright boo… I'm about to head on home."

That was her best bet. I was smooth on Shaneka. That bitch was green with envy. Talking about I could do better than a drug dealing killer, like she was out here fucking doctors and lawyers. Bitch please. She was fucking drug dealers and killers too.

*

"So, wassup? Your black ass coming to get me or what," I joked.

Not too long after Shaneka left, my neurologist came to visit me, and he cleared me for discharge. A bitch was so happy to be leaving.

As soon as he left, I rung my nurse, telling her to get me the fuck out of there. But before I could leave, they wanted me to walk around the unit on the crutches I was going home with, just to document my progress. I was good, and walking on them just fine, being that I had been walking around on them since I woke up from my coma.

"Right now?" he asked like he was preoccupied.

Before I could say anything, the sound of a bitch in the background grabbed my attention. Everybody knows how crazy about this nigga, even though this nigga ain't my nigga. I'd still shut a bitch down over him.

"Yeah nigga. Right now! What? You busy with a bitch or something," I snapped.

He chuckled and said, "Yo, I'm on my way shorty."

"Where you at? Who is that kee-keeing and ha-haing?"

"Is that your girl? Tell her I want a fucking refund. I've been waiting for my engagement photos for weeks now!"

It was Symphony. Hearing her annoying ass voice brought on every unpleasant memory I had of her. I was so pissed, that the grip I had on my phone was so lethal that I was sure it'd snap in half if I kept at it.

The moment the memory of my photography gigs came to me, I had Omni contacted every last one of my clients apologizing about the delay in things. She specifically told all of them that I had been in a serious accident. Now this bitch want to play dumb with me. I'd smack the shit out of her mad ass.

"Watch out," Cassim said to her.

"You with cha bitch huh? You know what nigga? Fuck you. I'll just call one of my brothers. I don't know why I called your weak ass—Hello?!"

He hung up on me and I sat up on side of the bed with flaring nostrils, calling him back. But he sent me to voicemail. He was doing me dirty again. Ignoring me, making me feel like shit. I swear, when he gets here I'm popping him right in his mouth.

Yo why in the hell do I even care? Really though... I was bugging. Straight up playing myself by loving him as much as I do when he couldn't give a fuck less about me.

I wish it was easy for me to just walk away. I wish I could just wave him off like I'd do any other nigga. But Cassim wasn't just any ol' nigga. He was *that* nigga. He had me so gone that although I knew I was going bat shit crazy, I kept at it anyway. I couldn't control it; it was what he did to me.

I called him again and this time he answered.

I yelled, "Hello—

"Stop yelling. Stop overreacting. Get yo shit together and wait for me. I'm on my way," he said before hanging up on me once again.

*

"Put a smile on that face, gorgeous," said Cassim, walking into the room just as my nurse was taking the IV out of my arm.

"I was just telling her that," said Nurse Becky, glancing over her shoulder at Cassim who was grabbing my bags for me.

"I don't have anything to smile about," I said with an attitude with my eyes narrowed at Cass.

He rubbed his eye with his freehand, "You breathing, aren't you?"

He knew why I was mad, and as usual, he thought it was funny. He secretly loved it when he made me crazy. His ass lucky the nurse was in here, otherwise I dead ass would have smacked him.

Smacking him wouldn't get me anything but drama. I didn't need drama. I needed to know what it was between us, on the real. I couldn't wait to get into the car with him. I needed to know what was up. I needed clarity.

Not knowing what we were was bugging me. Like I said, he's been a total sweetheart, but there was a pain in my chest that told me that was all going to change when I fully recovered.

"You have a lot to smile about, Ryann," said Nurse Becky, applying pressure to my arm after removing the IV. "You and your little one survived a life threatening accident, your memory is improving by the hour, your leg will be completely healed in about three weeks, and to top it off, you're getting out of here. And this nice gentleman has been catering to your every need. Now, what is there to be frowning about?"

Oh, you mean besides the fact that the man I'm madly in love with broke up with me? What is there to frown about... hmm.. let's see... The man you speak so highly of wasn't much of a gentleman the day before my accident. Not to mention, days prior he'd called me a bitch and had me carried out of his house.

Outside of all of the fucked up shit I just ran down, I did have a lot to be thankful for. Still, I didn't have the urge to smile. My heart was broken, and I felt like the man who was responsible had been toying with it since I've been in here.

Walking in calling me gorgeous. Helping me on and off the bedpan when I was just in too much pain to sit on the commode. Bringing me food. Holding me through the night. Telling me he loved me every chance he got. Knowing that once time progressed this would all be just something in the past. I was so confident that everything would change because the look in his eyes were different. That twinkle was missing.

"You're right," I said with a forced smile.

Fifteen minutes later, I was being pushed out of the hospital in a wheelchair. Aside from my gloomy mood, the weather was absolutely gorgeous. The sun was shining brightly, with not a cloud in sight. I really wanted to go downtown by the water to get some shots of the sun beating against the river.

Shortly after Cassim got me settled, he got into the car as well.

"What's up with you and Symphony," I immediately asked, not ready to dead the subject.

He put his seatbelt on and glanced at me, "Same thing that was up weeks ago. Shit."

"Yeah okay, Cassim. I'm clowning. I don't give a fuck about what you got going on. You ain't my dude," I said with my arms crossed over my chest.

"You sure you don't give a fuck? Sure sound like there is a little fuck given, sweetheart," said Cass with a smirk as he pulled away from the hospital.

I wanted him to say something about the comment I made about him not being my nigga. But he didn't. All that was to me, was confirmation. We weren't together and probably never would be again.

Since he said nothing about the comment I made, I left the whole subject of 'what are we' alone. I had my answer.

Chapter 7 – Cass

"What are you about to do," asked Ryann when I pulled up in front of her house.

"Handle some business. Unless you need something," I said with raised eyebrows.

She shrugged and licked her lips, "Nah, I'm good."

Ryann wasn't good, she was still pissed about Symphony being in the background when she called earlier.

I tried to control a lot of shit in my life, but unfortunately, no one can control what mafuckas around them do. Ryann needed to understand that. Shorty went bat shit crazy every time a bitch batted her eyelash or smiled at me. Fuck did she want me to do? Isolate myself from the rest of the world?

I was kicking it at Luck's shit, handling business when Symphony brought her slut ass over to where we were to talk.

She had been on my dick tough since she found out about Ryann and me breaking up. Dead ass wasting her time though. Just like she wasted her time that night she tried to fuck me.

She was able to get my dick hard, and even slid a condom down over it. But the moment she went to lower her pussy down over it, it went soft. She didn't do it for me. No one could do it for me. No one, but Ryann. Since I met her, she's the only one I saw. The only one who could turn me on in the simplest ways.

Symphony was in her feelings heavy that night too. She cried and all that. I was drunk as fuck, but I did remember her saying she had been trying to fill the void of losing me for years. She couldn't believe that I was in love with someone and I never loved her. Some ol' emotional shit I couldn't give a fuck less about.

I shifted the car in park and hopped out to help her up to the house. Juice and Adrien jogged down the stairs, and slapped hands with me. Adrien opened the passenger door, helping Ryann out while I grabbed her belongings bag and medicine from the backseat.

"Hit me up if you need anything, sweetheart," I said to Ryann as Adrien helped her sit on the couch.

She frowned in pain and nodded, "Alright."

I ran my tongue over my bottom lip and scratched the back of my head, "Yo, I love you aight?"

Her eyebrows snapped together and she giggled, "I love you too, Cass."

I did love baby. She knew that. I just barely verbalized it. Every now and then though, I wanted her to hear it. Especially when she was tripping about bitches like anybody besides her mattered. Regardless of whatever we're going through, Ryann will always be special to me.

*

"If you ain't pulling up on me to tell me who it was that lied on me, you might as well hop back in that whip and scur off bruh," I said to Scotty before taking a long pull from the blunt I had pinched between my thumb and index finger.

Scotty ran his hand over his blond hair and approached me with a smirk on his face, "I've got something better."

"Fuck is better than the name of a rat, Scott," I asked with a chuckle.

We were meeting on the east side of Detroit in the parking lot of Mandees Bar and Grill. I'd just finished chopping it up with Freddie and was getting ready to hit the crib when Scotty called me about linking.

Scotty looked over his shoulder at his car and yelled, "Come on."

Seconds later, the passenger door opened, and *she* stepped out. My right eye twitched and I angrily chuckled, "Nigga, you out cha fucking mind or what?"

I balled my fist and stood towering over Scotty who stood there with his hands up, "Look man, she just wants to talk."

As she approached us, she wore a crooked smile while smoothing her hair over. She looked clean. Her clothes were ironed, her teeth were brushed, and she had on a decent pair of shoes. She wore a weave, and her face wasn't as dry and blistered up as it was the last time she walked up on me.

I didn't give a fuck about any of that though. I wanted this bitch from around me.

"Hi Cassim—"

"Mothafucka. Call me what you called me," I said staring down at her with tight lips and a mug. "What I tell you I'd do to you if I saw you again? Bitch you thought I was bluffin?"

The last time I saw the woman who birthed me, I told her if I saw her I would choke the life out of her.

I took one last pull from my blunt and flicked it out of my fingers before approaching her. Scotty jumped in between us, with his hands out, trying to stop me from doing harm to her. He couldn't stop me. No one could stop me. I didn't give a shit about the traffic, or the people going in and out of Mandee's. All I wanted was for this bitch to stop breathing. I wanted her dead.

It was her fault. Everything I endured as a child. It was her fault I couldn't move past the shit Ryann did. As badly as I wanted to let go of what she did, I couldn't. As much as I tried not to let my past influence my present, it did, and I hated it.

Every time I considered forgiving Ryann, I'd think of all of the times I forgave 'her'. She'd come home, I'd smile brightly, ready to forgive her for leaving me alone for days, and then she'd toss unappetizing food at me, call me everything but my name, and leave again. I couldn't trust people because of her.

I thought that if I forgave Ryann, she would eventually betray me again. I didn't need that type of shit in my life. I didn't need that kind of burden. I'd probably fuck around and do something I'd regret if I gave Ryann a second chance and she did me dirty. I'd kill her. I didn't want to kill Ryann. But if she betrayed my trust again, I would. So, instead of chancing it, I'd rather push her away.

I pushed Scotty away, steady marching towards her.

"I just wanted to—

I cut her off midsentence by wrapping my hand around her throat. She didn't fight back. She let me choke her. I didn't give a fuck about the tears rolling down her face as I choked her harder.

Why would I? Did she care about the tears rolling down my face when she repeatedly abandoned me? Did she give a fuck about the horrible conditions I was forced to live in because she didn't want to be a mother? What about the damage she was doing to me mentally? She didn't give a flying fuck about that. So, why should I care about what I'm doing to her?

Honor thy mother and father, huh? Or my days will be shortened, huh? At this point, it was fuck the bible. It was fuck thy mother and father. Because it had always been fuck me.

"Cassim—

"Get in the car and pull off, Scotty."

"Ryann's pregnant. If there is anything worth saving yourself for, it's that," said Scotty reminding me of the future of my own kid.

If I recklessly killed this bitch, I'd for sure be spending the rest of my life in jail. My child would be forced to grow up without a father like I was. I didn't want that for my kid.

I flung the bitch away from my grip and walked away. She stumbled and fell back onto the hard pavement, gasping for air.

"Keep your nose out of my business, Scotty. Worry about finding your own fucking parents. Worry about patching your own shit. Keep yo focus on what's important nigga. Like, that name," I said as I walked away.

"I just want a do over, Cassim," she yelled, with tears pouring from her eyes. "Please son, forgive me."

In response, I slammed my car door. I sat behind the wheel of my car with flaring nostrils, gripping the steering wheel, heart beating wildly, breathing heavily.

Seeing her took me back to those times. Those dark times in my life. As a child, alone in a dark house with no water, no food, and no heat for the cold winter months. Hungry, crying, and confused. Wondering, why I wasn't loved. Wondering if the next time she came by if she would give me a bath. Wondering if she'd stay with me next time. Wondering if she was going to love me the way the woman in my dream did.

I got my answer when I was taken away and she never came looking for me. Now that I'm a grown ass man and she's full of regret, I'm supposed to forgive her? Fuck that bitch.

Chapter 8 – Ryann

A month later

"Again, I apologize about the delay," I said to one of my clients after handing her, her photos.

She waved me off, "It's totally fine, Ryann. I'm just glad that you're okay."

I was out and about, taking care of business I had been neglecting during my recovery. After making four deliveries, it was time for me to drop Symphony's photos off to her and her fiancé. I purposely saved her for last. I had been trying to avoid drama all together these days, so I made her my last stop.

Mrs. Duncan and I parted ways and I climbed back into my car. Pulling my phone from my pocket, I got a glimpse of the time. I had an hour and a half before the start of my first prenatal appointment. I was ecstatic. I couldn't wait to hear the sound of my baby's heart beat again, and I hoped that I'd be able to get some ultrasound pictures. I didn't care that the baby was only the size of a pea, I still wanted to see her.

I was hoping for a girl, Cassim didn't care either way. He was just happy to be having a baby.

Things between he and I were still the same. Cass was simply Cass. He wasn't *my* Cass.

Just as I expected, the moment I was released from the hospital things with Cassim switched. He was still nice... always a gentleman. But he made it very clear to me that we were nothing but friends... parents to the same kid. He didn't verbalize it, but I knew it by his actions.

I was going with the flow of things and just taking everything a day at a time. Not being with him still hurt, but I was coping. What other choice did I have? I was over begging him and trying to get him to see things from my perspective. I didn't even bring it up anymore.

I still loved him. I loved him with every fiber of my being. Every inch of me. I loved him with everything that made me, me. But if we couldn't be, then so be it. I had too much going on now to let Cassim not forgiving me consume my every thought. If he didn't want to be with me, then so be it. The only obligation he truly had was to be there for his child which he had been.

I scrolled through my contacts and called Symphony's fiancé, Todd. I had been in touch with him instead of Symphony. He was easier to talk to. I wanted to remain as positive as possible. They were busy though and couldn't meet me until after my doctor's appointment which pissed me the fuck off, being that we discussed me dropping the pictures off three days prior. Todd gave me their address, apologized, and told me to come by when I could.

*

"You think she really, permanently forgot," I heard Ashlee say when I walked into the house.

She was in her bedroom, with the door closed, obviously talking about me and that shit pissed me off. For the most part, I had most of my memory back. Sometimes I had to be reminded about stuff that happened in the past. And sometimes I forgot small stuff. Like, for example, I forgot about a hair appointment I had scheduled a week before the accident. It wasn't until my stylist called me the day of wondering where I was. It was the small stuff that I forgot.

But by the tone of Ashlee's voice, I could tell that whatever she was rapping me about, wasn't small. I tossed my MCM bag on the couch and headed for her bedroom. I knocked on it, and she opened, standing in a small crack between the frame and the door.

"Oh, hey Ry. When did you get back," she asked with a half-smile.

"Bitch, who you in there rapping me to," I said as I gave the door a hard push.

She stumbled back, and the door flew open. When I saw Juice sitting on side of her bed, I had a flashback. A flashback of catching them fucking. I immediately got sick to my stomach and threw up this morning's bacon, egg and cheese bagel.

"Ry—

I yelled, cutting Juice off, "Get the fuck out of my house! Both of you!"

I was devastated and disgusted. What kind of sick shit were they on? I had never in my life been so grossed out. They were casual about the shit too, like it was normal for them to be fucking. Like we didn't share the same bloodline. Like we didn't grow up together. We are family. Blood family!

Juice ran his hand over the top of his head and pushed himself up off the bed, "You still gone keep this between us, right?"

"Get the hell out of my face, Justice," I yelled. "You're worried about me telling Omniel, but you should be worrying about your mental stability. The both of you bitches. Nasty. Sick. Disgusting."

"Say what you want. You don't know shit. All you know is what you see! Gone and tell that bitch if you want to. I dare you. Try to ruin this shit if you want to, Ryann," yelled Ashlee.

Juice grabbed a handful of Ashlee's hair and pulled her by me, out of the room, "Shut the fuck up LeeLee."

"Let me go, Juice," she cried. "This ain't no sew-in nigga, you're ripping tracks out my head!"

"All I need to know is what I witnessed to know that you two are sick," I yelled, cupping my hand over my mouth, feeling the urge to throw up again.

Juice looked over his shoulder at me, "You gone let me explain—

"Fuck no! I don't want to hear it. I don't want to deal with either of you. Just go!"

*

"You ready," he asked over the other end of the phone.

"Yeah, here I come," I replied before hanging up.

Once Juice and Ashlee left, I calmed down and made myself a couple of peanut butter and jelly sandwiches. I had been on them bitches heavy since I got home from the hospital. That and ice cream. I told myself I was going to eat healthy so I wouldn't gain too much weight, but I ain't been eating shit but fattening foods.

I left out of the house and jogged down the stairs to Cassim's awaiting car. He stood outside of it, with the passenger door already open for me, with his phone to his ear.

A million butterflies fluttered in my stomach, as my heart rate picked up. He was so got damn fine in his red v-neck top, black jeans, and red and black Nike Foam's. His dreads were freshly touched up, and I could smell his cologne before I got to the car.

"Hey," I spoke.

He gave me a head nod, and I climbed into the car.

At first, those head nods made my heart skip beats. Because they would be accompanied by a lustful glare or that *'I found it'* look. These days, I hated that head nod because they were empty. He gave me head nods like I was just a regular bitch on the street.

He closed the door behind me and I buckled my seat belt. We were headed for my first OBGYN appointment and I was a little excited. Nah, not a little. I was extremely excited.

I never had anything against being pregnant. It's just that my last pregnancy had to be terminated. It was necessary—well, in my eyes it was. Fuck what anybody else has to say about it. Now, it was like I was given a second chance. With this second chance, would God bless Cassim and I with one as well?

He got in and shifted the car in drive, while holding his phone on his ear with his shoulder. I reached into my purse and pulled out a bag of M&M's. He glanced over at me and extended his hand for some. I looked down at it, huffed, and popped one into my mouth.

"Aight, G. We'll link a little later," he said before hanging up. "You being stingy with candy I bought?" he asked as he tossed it phone in the small compartment under where the radio sat.

"Fuck outta here, boasting over a dollar bag of candy," I said before fumbling through my purse for a dollar. "I can easily—

He cut me off, "Calm down. I'm just fuckin' with yo uptight ass."

"If I'm uptight, it's because I have a reason to be," I shot back.

I had been uptight and it was for a number of reasons. For one, we weren't together and hadn't even really discussed why. Two, I felt like he was fucking with that Symphony bitch... I mean, 'cause he sure ain't fucking me. And Three... good Lord I missed his black ass.

I missed him so much, despite the fact that I see him every single day. I missed him so much, despite the fact that I was just with him yesterday. I missed what we had. Spending time with him now wasn't the same as before. The passion was gone. I hated it. I hated it so much. Although he dropped by every day, he barely spent time with me. It was always to drop by to check on me, or to bring me something. Never to kick it.

He responded by turning the stereo on. I wanted to shut the radio off and scream at the top of my lungs about how he was treating me unfairly. I wanted to burst out into tears about how sorry I was, and about how much I missed him too. But I couldn't. My primary focus in all of this was to be strong. I wasn't just living for me now. And if Cassim truly wanted to be over, then so be it. I couldn't go into that deep depression again. I had to eat. I had to drink. I couldn't fall under depression because if I did, the baby would too.

As I said... I wasn't just living for Ryann anymore. And to fall into that deep dark hole I fall into as a result of missing Cassim... I couldn't go there. To go there would be selfish and heartless.

*

"You see it, dad?" asked my OBGYN, Dr. Oshea.

Cassim could see it. He didn't have to say that he did. I could see the happiness all in his eyes. He was never really big on showing emotion, but at this moment, he couldn't help himself. He smiled the biggest smile I'd ever seen on his face and nodded.

"Fuck," he mumbled before running his hand down over his face.

Dr. Oshea giggled, "The first baby always has an effect on you!"

"How far along is she?" asked Cassim, with his eyes locked on mine.

He was so happy a minute ago, but after Dr. Oshea said what she said, that smile was wiped right off his face. It wasn't our first baby. Well, it wasn't mine. I wasn't sure if it was Cassim's first or not. And sadly, not knowing if it was his or not didn't matter to him.

Dr. Oshea cleaned the gel off my belly, "She's ten weeks."

"When do we find out the sex of the baby," I asked.

Cassim shook his head, "I want to find out in the delivery room. Not before."

"Well, that's a conversation to be had. Right now, I just want to know when they can tell," I said with an attitude.

"Well, typically at twenty weeks," said Dr. Oshea, sensing the tension in the room.

The rest of the appointment was spent discussing the basics. The remainder of the appointment was awkward. I just knew the day would go to shit from there. And I was right.

*

"It's such a beautiful day. Perfect walking weather," I said, trying to lighten the mood.

The doctor's appointment was over, and we were walking to his car. He hadn't said anything to me and it was bugging me. Cassim use to be my happy place, but now, shit was so cold that I sometimes hated to be around him. He was holding a grudge and it was aggy as fuck.

"Hell yeah," he nonchalantly replied, as he texted on his phone.

I felt foolish, trying to indulge in conversation with someone who clearly didn't want to speak to me. It sort of amazed me how what I thought would happen after I was discharged was really happening. Although I had a feeling he would go back to being mean to me, I dreaded it. I wanted things to be the way they were when I was in the hospital. The smiles, the compliments.. the way he took care of me. The way he opened up to me… I missed it all.

It was clear to me that those feelings of fear had subsided and he just didn't give a fuck anymore. Was it that he didn't care anymore? Of had someone else caught his attention? Maybe it wasn't Symphony. What if he had found someone new?

The thought of that alone made my stomach turn, and a warm sensation to fill my chest. Fear. The fear of him replacing me. It scared the living shit out of me. Was that what had happened? He'd found another?

I stupidly stood outside of the car, expecting him to open the door up for me like he always did, but he didn't. His attention was placed on whoever he was texting. Again, my heart broke. He'd just held the door opened for me when he picked me up. Was this nigga really mad about the comment Oshea made? I hated that it was so hard for me to read him.

I licked my bottom lip and got into the car. As I was buckling my seatbelt, he pulled off.

"Oh could, you swing me over to one of my clients house to drop these photos off? It won't take long."

He nodded and I put the address in on my phone.

I didn't tell Cassim where I was dropping the pictures off at on purpose. If I would have told him I needed him to take me to Symphony's house before he dropped me off, he probably would have told me no, especially if they were back fucking around. I needed to see how he would react to seeing them together.

*

Fifteen minutes later, we were pulling up at Symphony's house. She was standing out on the porch with Todd, in a robe, watching Cassim park.

He huffed with a chuckle and a subtle shake of his head.

"What? You mad, home boy," I asked as I grabbed envelope with their photos in it from my oversized MCM bag.

"Is that what you thought would happen? That I'd get mad," he asked with his eyes locked on mine.

I shrugged, "I mean, you look a little mad—

"Fuck out of here with the childish shit, Ryann," said Cass before picking his phone up again. "Go handle yo business and stop acting like a fucking kid."

The corners of my mouth turned up into a frown as I hopped out of the car. Cassim wasn't mad. He was annoyed and it wasn't with Symphony and her dude standing on the porch waiting for me. He was annoyed with me. I didn't give a fuck, I was annoyed with his ass too.

The weather was a perfect eighty degrees, so I wore a cute floral wrap dress. My stomach was still fairly small, being that I was only ten weeks. I had a little pudge that was only noticeable if you were staring. And Symphony was staring, honey.

Sinn must have told her I was pregnant. Bitch looked green with envy. I wore a smile, although I wasn't happy to be seeing her. I was smiling because she looked mad as shit. She kept looking over at Cassim's car.

"Good afternoon, you two," I said with a smile before handing the pictures to Todd. "Here are your photos. Sorry for the delay—

Symphony snatched the envelope from my hands and said, "I will not be referring you to any of my friends. The way you do business is absolutely unacceptable. And you better hope my photos are of great quality."

"Now, honey," said Todd shaking his head.

I pointed at Symphony, "Keep being disrespectful, Symphony. Don't make me tell Todd why you're really mad!"

Symphony yelled, "Bitch he already know what it is! He know just like I know that you're mad because you think I still want Cassim's black, ugly ass. He knows ev-vor-ree-thang!"

I looked away with a smirk, wondering if I should pop this bitch in the mouth? I mean, she was disrespecting on a serious level. Disrespecting in ways I never tolerated. But then again, I am pregnant and Symphony's a spiteful type bitch. She'd probably kick me in the stomach.

Before I could react, I heard a car door slam. Looking over my shoulder, I took in Cassim approaching us. He was scowling, and he was clenching and unclenching his jaw. He was pissed.

He marched right by me, up to the top of the stairs. He looked down at Symphony and said, "Apologize."

He spoke to Symphony like her fiancé wasn't standing right next to them. Cassim didn't' give a fuck.

"Excuse me, man," said Todd with his hand out, in between Cassim and Symphony.

Cassim roughly slapped Todd's hand away and repeated with gritted teeth, "Apologize."

Symphony took a step back, tightening her robe, "Cassim, get the hell out of my face. Did I fell to mention that Todd was a police officer? You assault either of us—

"I give a fuck?" Cassim gestured towards me. "This beautiful young woman has been nothing but polite to you. Apologize. I won't tell you again."

Todd stood next to Symphony with his hands on his hips, like a bitch, letting Cassim disrespect his lady. No wonder Symphony was still so hung up on Cassim. Todd was clearly lacking.

Todd sighed, "Honey—

"I apologize," said Symphony with a smile. "Oh, and Cassim? I'm sorry for your loss. I heard about the baby. I know how much you love children, so I know you're just devastated!"

I charged at Symphon, and Cassim stopped me before I could knock the bitch on her ass. I was about sick and tired of Symphony's shit. She was trying to hurt Cassim and he knew it. But, hurting him would only cause more conflict between him and I. She knew that shit too.

I hocked up a glob of spit and spat at her. It landed right on her forehead and she went crazy.

"Lock her up, Todd! Put her in jail right now for assault," she screamed while she wiped my spit from her forehead with the sleeve of her robe.

I didn't give a fuck about Todd being a cop. I didn't give a fuck about spitting being assault either. I couldn't put hands on her, but I could for sure disrespect her.

I hocked up more spit and Cassim said, "Stop." Before I could spit it at her.

His voice was stern as he carried me away from the house. He meant business, so I swallowed the spit. Symphony was steady on the porch screaming for her fiancé to lock me up. Poor Todd waved his hand and walked into the house, while his bitch threw a whole fit.

Cassim put me in the car and slammed the door on me. I didn't want to be alone with him right now. I didn't want to be in the same car with him. I knew what I was about to get the whole ride to my house and I didn't want to sit through that agony. The agony of his anger brought on by being reminded about the abortion not once, but twice today.

Seconds later, Cassim got into the car and sped from in front of the house

"So, you don't want to talk about the shit, ever Cassim?" I asked breaking the awkward silence in the car.

He had been quiet since we pulled off from in front of Symphony's about five minutes ago.

"Talk about what"" he asked, scowling.

"About the... About the abortion—"

He glanced at me with a chuckle and cut me off, "Did you feel like the conversation was one to have before I found out, darlin—"

"Stop calling me that shit, nigga," I yelled pointing my finger in his face.

He shook his head and ran his tongue over his bottom lip, "Yo, chill with the pointing and shit, Ryann."

"What you gone do nigga? Put me out of your car the same way you put me out of your house? Just because I want to talk? Just like I did that day. Almost two months later and you're still running away from that talk. On some coward shit."

He sighed and ran his hand over his head. He didn't say anything, but that scowl stayed on his face. Everything was going fine until Dr. Oshea said we were first time parents. And then for that stupid bitch Symphony to blatantly try to joke about the shit only added fuel to an ignited fire.

At least before the appointment, he was talking to me and he didn't have that look on his face. Now, he looked utterly disgusted, the same way he looked when we broke up.

"I think that's some true ass sucka shit on the real. Shit, when you thought I was about to die, and that I had forgotten you, you were dead ass loving a bitch. Holding me, telling me you loved me, telling me everything there is to know about yourself. Fuck is it now? Nothing. You're a fucking fraud. You sold me a dream, and I let you," I yelled.

"Call it what you want, sweetheart," he said as he stopped at a stop sign. "What happened had me shook. I can admit that. That shit you pulled? Straight disloyal. I have no tolerance for disloyalty. You know what the fuck it is. Stop acting brand new. I can never trust you again."

I slammed my phone in my purse and yelled, "I was fucking raped, Cassim! Raped! And then I ended up pregnant! The baby probably wasn't even yours! Do you understand that shit!?"

"Yo, you feeling alright? You wylin out shorty. Like I did some ho shit behind your back."

"It's not what I think you did behind my back, nigga! It's that fucking dream you sold me when I was in the hospital. I knew shit would flip. But then again, I thought that maybe... just maybe things would go back to the way they were before. Now look at you... sitting there like I mean nothing. Fuck you, Cassim." I said waving my hand at him, "And nigga, I don't know what the fuck you did behind my back. You screaming loyal shit, but who's to say you wasn't out here doing me dirty? You and that ho Symphony seemed mighty upset a minute ago."

He glanced at me, sucked his teeth with a frown and said, "You sound stupid as fuck. Just talkin' crazy cause you ain't got shit smart to say. Shut that foo-foo shit up."

He was right. I didn't have anything to say. I knew there was nothing between Symphony and him. I was just trying to defend myself. I knew that during our relationship, Cassim was honest and faithful. But I still talked my shit. I wouldn't be a woman if I didn't.

"Yeah whatever nigga. You shut the fuck up. If it ain't that goofy bitch, someone else definitely got your attention. You've been on some high horse for a month now."

"Fuck outta here. You know damn well a nigga ain't got eyes for nobody but you."

I rolled my eyes and sucked my teeth, "Yeah, aight." I fingered through my curly hair and said, "You talk good."

All I wanted to do was to truly move past the whole abortion thing. He was truly milking the situation, to be honest. Cassim tends to harbor ill feelings when a person does him wrong, so in a sense, I understood him. I just couldn't understand how he couldn't understand my reasoning for it in the first place.

"How can we move past this, Cassim? I'm not asking for a relationship...I'm just asking for forgiveness."

"I've forgiven you," he said, staring at me with so much intensity that it was almost as if he was staring through me.

"Stop frowning, Cassim," I said. "If you've forgiven me as you say you have... you wouldn't be staring at me with a frown on your face."

"I wear this frown because," he looked away and chewed on the inside of his cheek before saying. "You fuckin hurt a nigga, Ryann. You think I would react like this every time I'm reminded of the abortion?"

As soon as the words left his mouth, he immediately covered it like he didn't mean for what he thought to come out the way it did. He didn't like to show emotion. He didn't like to show anything remotely close to weakness. And in that moment, he felt like he was weak. But he wasn't. His honesty was utterly beautiful. Heartbreakingly beautiful.

The pain I felt in my chest when he said it was indescribable. I'd hurt a man who once told me he didn't care about living or dying. I hurt a man who walked around like he was invincible. Men like Cass... they don't hurt easily. Damn. How much damage had I done?

The decision I made, was made alone. I knew it was selfish. I knew I should have talked to him before I did it, but I didn't. I selfishly lied on that table and let them suck the baby out of me. I was selfish. To me, Cassim was like a God—indestructible. Hard, and someone who could possibly move mountains. A man like Cassim? Psssh. They couldn't be hurt. But I was wrong.

I thought Cassim was angry. But I was wrong. He was hurt.

I unbuckled my seatbelt and reached over across the arm rest. I grabbed hold of him and wrapped my arms around him as much as they would allow. He didn't hug me back though. He sat there, unmoving, like a statue.

"Wrap your arms around me, Cassim," I said into the crook of his neck.

And he did.

He wrapped his arms around me in return. He hugged me so tight that I felt like I would possibly break into two. There were so many unspoken words just by the intensity of his hug.

He took a deep breath and I kissed him. I kissed him on his cheek and you know what he did? He grabbed the sides of my face and kissed me on the lips. I wrapped my arms around his neck and deepened the kiss. Being strong didn't matter anymore. I wanted to feel his tongue dance around my mouth. I needed this. I needed this so bad. I was so hungry for his tongue… so turned on by our kiss, that I began to moan into his mouth.

But then… he pulled away from me and drove off from the stop sign. I felt stupid. The admittance of his pain had pulled so many emotions out of me that I stupidly crossed a line I had been trying to avoid for a month.

I swallowed and sat back down in my seat. I sat there, staring straight ahead while tears slowly trickled down my face. I was being weak again. I hated this shit.

Chapter 9— Cass

She forgot to buckle her seatbelt back up. So, I stopped in the middle of the road and buckled it up for her. She tensed up when I reached over and sighed. I didn't know what to do with myself when it came to Ryann. I didn't know if I wanted to hug her, kiss her... or if I wanted to stay the fuck away from her.

"Are you hurting me because I hurt you," she asked with tears running down her face.

Beep! Beep!

I looked through the rearview mirror and pulled off.

To deliberately hurt her would be some sucka shit. I wasn't trying to hurt her. I was trying *not* to hurt her.

I've always had a hard time trusting people, which was why I didn't. But Ryann didn't fall under the category of 'people'. Shorty was a piece of me. The piece of me that had a beating heart. The piece of me that gave a fuck. Which is why her betrayal fucked with me so much.

She wanted me to understand her decision. Hell, I never gave the situation any thought. All I saw was red when I got that phone call about her getting an abortion. I prayed like hell that the person who told me was lying, and just trying to break up what I had with Ryann. When shorty confirmed that what I was told was the truth, I didn't give a damn about why. All I cared about was how she kept that away from me.

Trying to explain to her why I was the way I was would be pointless. She would never understand it. She would only think that I was trying to hurt her, and I truly wasn't.

"My intentions aren't to hurt you, Ryann," I finally replied.

Shorty was sitting over there damn near going crazy. She couldn't keep her hands out of her hair, her knee was bouncing profusely, and she kept fidgeting with the puffy ball on her keychain.

"Well that's what you're doing," she said, looking down into her lap at nothing.

Hurting her was the last thing I wanted to do. I wanted to pull this car over and grab her. I wanted to sit her in my lap and kiss on her lips. But I couldn't. The burdens of my childhood kept me from giving into my deep need of her. I didn't like to be let down. I stopped giving a fuck about the things she made me care about, long ago. Ryann had brought up feelings I buried. She made me feel in ways I never wanted to feel again. Feelings I had warranted out of my life when I was a child. To have that feeling of being wanted, that feeling of true ass love… it felt wonderful. Until I found out she had an abortion. That shit killed me.

"Pull this car over," she demanded.

I kept driving. And her crazy ass grabbed the steering wheel, and turned it to the right, making the car swerve. I snatched the wheel from her grips and yelled, "What the fuck you doing?!"

"Pull this bitch over, Cassim," she yelled at the top of her lungs. "You acting like a true ass bitch right now! Like a pussy ass nigga." She was talking mad greasy. Her lips were turned down and all that like she was on some real savage shit.

"Man, you fuming and shit, so I'mma let that lil' disrespect slide."

"Nigga, fuck you!"

I laughed, "Yooo."

She grabbed the door handle, ready to jump out, but I quickly hit the locks. She was tripping. Her chest was heaving and she was beating on the dashboard, screaming about me not being fair, saying that I wasn't listening. She was screaming and crying about how all she wanted to do was talk.

So, I pulled over and let her.

I killed the engine and scratched my head, "Speak."

She sat up, unbuckled her seatbelt, and turned her body around to face me, "Look at me, Cassim."

I sighed and turned to face her.

She cupped my face with her hands and said, "I fucked up, aight—"

"We got pass that part already, sweetheart. Get to the shit I haven't heard already."

She frowned and said, "Whhhhy... Whhyyy are you doing this shit?"

"I told you why. You know how I move, Ryann. I need honesty and you didn't give me that."

She pulled her hands away and balled her fist up. I stuck my chin out, daring her to rock my shit, but she didn't. Instead she punched the palm of her hand with a menacing laugh.

"Yoooo... is this shit really happening right now? What type of fucked up person are you?"

"The type of fucked up person you fell in love with. Stop trying to throw dirt on my name just because a nigga ain't feeling the way you did shit behind my back. Kill the victim shit. I forgave your black ass, what the fuck else do you want from me, Ryann?"

Her nostrils flared with anger as she said, "Look me in the eyes and tell me that you don't want to be with me anymore. Look me in the eyes and tell me that you don't love me Cassim."

I locked eyes with her and lied.

I lied to protect myself. I'd been abandoned and done wrong far too many times to let the shit happen again.

"That shit is dead. So, buckle ya fucking seat belt up and stop throwing tantrums, like you don't know you carrying my seed."

The pain behind her brown eyes ate at me. But she stopped having her tantrum, sat straight ahead, and adjusted her twisted seat belt.

She didn't say anything for the rest of the ride to the crib. The tears had stopped, the bouncing of her knee had seized... she was sitting there calm, cool, and collective like she didn't just grab the steering wheel on some nut shit.

Twenty minutes later, I pulled up on the block, in front of her house and shifted the car in park.

"You need anything?" I asked as she unbuckled her seatbelt.

She looked over her shoulder, "Nope."

Right after, she hopped out without a simple goodbye.

*

I pulled up behind Luck's whip and hopped out.

He was chilling on the hood of his car waiting on me. I hoped like fuck he had some information for me. The people in my corner had been coming up short lately when it came to supplying me with information I needed, and I was about sick of it. Usually Luck would have been had something for me. But it's been a whole month and I still didn't know who had hit shorty.

I knew very well that it could have truly been an accident, but I gave no fucks about that. Whoever hit her had no remorse, and I planned on having no remorse when I snatched the life out of them. I wouldn't give a fuck if the person behind the wheel had been a senior citizen. All I cared about was getting at whoever it was that hit baby and drove off on her like she meant nothing.

I approached him with an open palm and he slapped hands with me.

"What's good, G?"

Luck ran his hands down his face, "Shit crazy right now fam."

I hopped on the hood of his car next to him and asked, "What?"

"Yasmin pregnant. Sinn gone kill me dead."

I let out a gust of air and shook my head, "I need you to keep your head in the game though, Luck." I narrowed my eyes at him, "Don't let your personal shit interfere with what the fuck we got going on, you hear me?"

I was surprised to hear about Luck getting another bitch pregnant, but at the same time, I didn't give a fuck.

He shook his head, "Have I ever let my personal shit throw me off, nigga?"

"What's that word on that footage then nigga? I've been waiting for a week!"

He glanced at me and shook his head, "Bitch in her feelings and all 'lat. She purposely taking a long time to hack into the cameras—

"Make it right, Luck," I said, pointing at him. "Bow down to that bitch. Eat pussy and ass... I don't give a fuck what... make it right."

Luck laughed and said, "Fuck outta here, famo. A niggas not licking the dook-shoot. Fuck I look like?"

I laughed and said, “Shit nigga, you’d be surprised. If yo bitch clean, the bootyhole is sweet. Taste just as good as the—"

“Come on, G,” he yelled, cutting me off.

I laughed again, throwing my head back a little, “Look bruh. Just fix it. The next time I ask you about that footage, I want you to respond with video footage.”

Chapter 10 – Ryann

Knock. Knock. Knock.

"Ryann," sang Omni, slowly pushing my bedroom door open.

Since I got my memory back, I've been cool on her. Before the accident, I wasn't speaking to her. So, yeah, that's where I'm at with it. Her telling Cassim about that abortion ruined our friendship just as much as it ruined my relationship. I still didn't know if she had really told him, but I was confident that it was her.

"Did I say come in? The fuck?"

I was in a bad mood because of the fight Cassim and I had the other day. I tried to push it all to the back of my mind, but I couldn't. He literally looked me in the eyes and told me he was done with me. That shit hurt me. He said he wasn't trying to hurt me, but that is exactly what he did.

So, since he hurt me, I've been cool on him. A niggas got one time to hurt me, but I've given Cassim plenty. Just because I loved him. And the love I had for him made me senseless. Now though, I was playing the game just the way he wanted me to. He told me what we had was dead, so it was dead. I still had a hard time adjusting, but I was trying.

"Bitch you just mean," said Omni, opening my blinds. "Why are you in bed? It's a beautiful day—"

"You got a head injury too," I asked, pointing at her.

She frowned, "What—no… What are you talking about?"

She sat at the foot of my bed, frowning, wondering what I meant.

"I mean, you must have a mild case of amnesia or something... I'm good on you."

"You still on that stupid shit?" Omni sighed, "Be realistic, Ryann. Why in the fuck would I tell Cass you had an abortion?"

I shrugged, "Shit, probably because I knew Juice was cheating and didn't tell you. You could have done it out of spite. I would blame Nek but what would be her point of telling him?"

Mentioning Juice made me sick to my stomach all over again. Omniel didn't know what she had gotten herself into. I needed to tell her, but telling her would be an embarrassment to my family. She just needed to leave him the fuck alone. And not just because of what I knew about Juice and Ashlee. Because period! He was thee absolute fucking worst.

Omni drew back, "What? Nek? Bitch you didn't even tell Nek!"

"If I didn't tell her, how did she know..."

As I was talking, realization sat in. I didn't tell Nek shit!

"Hol up...hol up...hol up," I repeated over and over again, tripping.

"Ryannnn... you did not tell Shaneka you had an abortion. If she knows about it, she must've been eavesdropping that day you were yelling and shit about it."

I cocked my head to the side and squinted my eyes, "Buuuuut..."

I was so confused. Nothing made sense. But as I sat there thinking about everything that transpired that day, everything started to become just a little more clear. I hated that after a month, my memory was still a little foggy. It was expected, but still I hated it.

I knew exactly what Omni was talking about. I had gone off on her about the way she flaked on me and I mentioned the abortion. I was so in my feelings that I was yelling, not realizing I was putting all of my business out there. Anybody that was there that day could have told Cassim. But I was sure it was Nek. Simply because right after that shit happened, she asked to see my phone. Claiming that she couldn't find hers and wanted to use mine to call it. All along she was probably getting Cassim's number right out of my phone book.

I chewed on my bottom lip, fighting back tears. Shit between Nek and I had really gotten bad. I didn't know why she was doing this. I didn't do anything to this bitch. Why did she have it out so bad for me? Because I beat her ass? I mean what? What would really push her to the point to try to break up what I had with Cass?

"Aw naw, boo," said Omni scooting down the bed. She wrapped her arms around my trembling body, trying to calm me down.

But at this point, there wasn't any calming me down. All I saw was red. This bitch was really sitting on my porch, drinking and smoking like she wasn't a shady bitch. Out there entertaining a few dope boys in the hood. Fucking hood rat ass bitch.

"Watch out, Om. Let me up," I said before rubbing my lips together.

"For what?" asked Omni with raised eyebrows. "You cannot go out there trying to fight that bitch. Did you forget you are with child?"

"Who said anything about fighting, Omniel? Let me go."

As soon as Omniel let go of me, I hopped out of that bed and marched right out of the room. I headed down to her room and barged in. I placed my arm on the top of her dresser, and pushed everything on top of it, into her clothing bin. I didn't give a fuck that most of her perfume was in glass bottles, breaking, and spilling all over her clothes. I damn sure didn't care about the opened bottle of baby oil that had fallen on top neither.

"You just gone stand there? Or are you gonna help me get this bitch out of my house Omniel?"

Omni gave me the side eye, uncrossed her arms and helped me grab Shaneka's belongings, "This all you doing right? You ain't about to go out there trying to scrap are you?"

"Nah, I'm not."

Omniel had every right not to believe that. I didn't take disrespect lightly, and me just letting Nek walk away didn't sound right. I wasn't going to fight that bitch though.

"What are you doing, Ryann," yelled Shaneka while I tossed her shit out of the house out onto the lawn.

"Figure it out, you fluke ass bitch," I spat with my mouth turned down in disgust.

I was so upset that I was trembling. I had never seen a hating bitch like her before. And I've had my share of haters. The hate hurt more when it comes from someone you love. It hurt even more since it was Shaneka doing me dirty. I would expect some shit like this from LeeLee.

She stood up and passed the blunt to the dude she was sitting on, before approaching me. But Omniel stepped in front of me and shook her head no, "Just gone on, Nek. Don't even tempt her."

Nek was on some true tough shit, trying to show off in front of the gang of niggas she had in front of my house. She was running her dick suckers about how I needed to go grab her shit off the grass, meanwhile, I had taken my ass right back into the crib for more.

"One of you bitches will be picking my shit up. The fuck is she on," I heard Shaneka yell.

I pushed the storm door open and flung another one of her raggedy ass duffle bags over the railing, "You see what I'm on, ho. What's good? You want at me? Get at me."

She was trying to bitch me and I hated that shit. I wanted to beat her face into the pavement.

"Wooooow, I don't even know what this shit is about," she yelled with a chuckle. "This bitch wilding!"

"You know exactly what this shit is about," said Omni, steady blocking Nek's path into the house with her arms crossed over her chest.

"Shit, I know too," said one of the hustlers under his breath with a cough.

"What was that," I said with my top lip turned up. "What you just say?"

"Yo, I said nothing, Queen Cass," he said with his hands up.

I squinted and pointed in his face, "What the fuck did you just say?"

I was bugging. I knew exactly what he just said, I just wanted him to repeat it. So, what? I was out here looking stupid? Who else knew this bitch had ran her mouth about my personal business? Who all knew I had an abortion? I felt sick to my stomach, as my eyes roamed the ten to fifteen guys sitting and standing around my porch. Did they all know?

"The hell you running yo mouth for, nigga," said one of the guys shaking his head.

"You need to shut the fuck up, Nino," said Nek pointing her finger in his face. She turned to me and whispered, "This is about me telling him about the abortion? Come on now, Ry!"

Nino sucked his teeth and stood up, "Bitch you shut the fuck up. You a whole fraud out chea! You know what the fuck ma talm'bout. Smiling in shorty's face, knowing you were legit trying to fuck her nigga not too long ago. Begging boss to join in on the train we ran on yo rat ass."

"Aw shit," said Omniel.

I cocked my head back with laughter, in total disbelief. This bitch wanted my nigga. That's why she was running her mouth to him. I was so thrown off by this shit that I was literally cracking up. I was cracking up, and trembling, while Omni tried to calm me down.

What have I done to deserve all of this pain? First the shit with Dinero, then everything that followed. The accident, losing my memory… and now this? I just found out she was the one who told Cassim about the abortion, just to find out she tried to fuck him right after?

All I want is a break. I was supposed to be focused on getting my life in order for my baby, not drama. For a second there, I did think I would be drama free. Things were smooth sailing up until Cass and I got into it. Drama had come back with a vengeance. I didn't want to keep going through shit. I didn't want to keep getting hurt by people in my life.

Nothing was right. Everything was so fucking wrong man. I was not supposed to be here. I was supposed to sitting comfortably in Cassim's nice ass mansion. And if it wasn't for this fake ass bitch, I would be. I wouldn't be on the block. I wouldn't be going through any of the shit I was going through. What Cassim and I had wouldn't be 'dead' as he put it. Our relationship would be striving.

Nek use to be my ace. How in the fuck did we get here? I was fucking livid.

Finally, I got the laughing under control. Then... I snapped.

I turned around, went back into the house, snatched the drawer to the end table open, and grabbed my gun. I then cocked the hammer back and marched my ass right back outside. In that short period of time though, the dope boys had scattered like roaches and Cassim was walking up the porch.

I ignored him. I ignored Omni telling me to put the gun away. I ignored the tears streaming down Nek's face. And I ignored the fact that the block was crowded and all eyes were on the crazy girl with the gun pointed in her cousins face.

Ain't that Cass shorty? She on one," I heard someone across the street yell. *"Yoooo, that's shorty we ran a train on ain't it? The one who was begging to fuck with bruh. Shorty found out!?"*

Cassim approached me with his hand out, "Ryann, give me the gun."

I flinched away from his touch, "Don't... don't touch me nigga!"

Just as much as Shaneka was in the wrong, he was too. How did he fail to mention the fact that my cousin was begging to fuck him? Where was the loyalty? That loyalty he spoke so high of… where was it then? You think I would have held that information away from him? Shit no. The moment one of his dudes would have tried to get on, I would have called him. But he didn't call me. He didn't even tell me. And on top of that, he let this bitch ruin us. He gave her the satisfaction she wanted—to see us a part. All because she couldn't have him.

"You really want to do this right now, sweetheart," he said, slightly bent down, into my ear.

Again, I jerked away from him. I was utterly disgusted with Cassim at this point. I didn't think that I could ever have these type of feelings for him. But I did and they were raw as hell.

"Please, Ryann," cried Shaneka. "Please."

"Babe," said Omni. "You are pregnant. If you shoot this bitch… your baby will grow up without a mother. Come on Ryann.. you don't want that. I know you don't."

Omni was right. I didn't want that. And I didn't want my cousin to be so dirty either. What outweighed the other? The undying urge to split this bitches wig, or the importance of my baby growing up with me? I knew what it was like to grow up without my mother. And at the rate Cassim is going, he or she will probably grow up without him either. Growing up without parents hurt. In so many ways, Cassim and I were similar. We knew how much it hurt not to have parents. I never wanted that for my kid. Ever.

My eyes averted away from Nek, and I finally scanned the crowd in the street. Everybody was watching. Old people, young people, people I didn't know, people I didn't like. Everyone. In that thick crowd of people could lie a snake. A fucking snitch. One of them was because one of them were responsible for Cassim being locked up. They couldn't do shit with him because his alibi had checked out. But with me? They could do a lot.

"Why did you do it, Nek," I asked with a shaky voice, gun still pointed in her face.

She shook her head, crying ugly tears. Face scrunched up, drenched in tears and snot. She was petrified. She'd been shot before, but never close range. Never like this. She knew, that in that moment, I had her life in my hands.

But my life, and the life of my child's was far more important. At this point, I just wanted Shaneka away from me. I didn't care to hear why she did what she did. I already knew what it was. Jealousy.

She started to speak, but I grabbed the barrel of the gun, and hit her across the face with the butt of it.

"Daaaaaaamn," said everyone in the crowd, in unison.

"I think she broke my fucking nose," yelled Shaneka cupping her hand over her bleeding nose.

I then walked away, with slumped over shoulders, and tears rolling down my face. Both Omni and Cassim followed behind me. I told them that I just wanted to be left alone. Omni told me she loved me and left. But Cassim? He stayed.

BANG! BANG! BANG!

"Let me in to get the rest of my shit," yelled Shaneka.

I sat on the couch and threw my head back with my eyes closed, feeling myself about to lose it.

I heard the front door open, and then Cassim's voice came alive again.

"Yo, darlin... you want me to let shorty split cha fuckin wig? Get the fuck from around here, ma."

Shaneka didn't say anything. She knew better not to. Seconds later, the front door slammed again and the floor creaked with every step he took towards me. I wanted to yell out and tell him to leave. I wanted to punch him in the face, too. But I did nothing. I sat there, wishing I could do something to ease the pain of my broken heart, but there was nothing that could fix that. Once upon a time, Cassim could fix all of the pain in my life. These days, he was the cause of it.

"Ryann," he called out to me.

"Cassim, I asked you to leave. So, please do just that."

I kept my eyes closed. I had to. Because if I opened them, and he was staring at me, I would lose my voice. I didn't want to lose my voice. I didn't want to be weakened. In this moment, I needed to be strong. And the only way I could be strong right now was with my eyes closed.

"Do you need—"

"I need you to leave. Plain and simple."

*

"Ry baby, you up?"

I woke up to the smell of breakfast, and Goose knocking on my bedroom door.

"Yeah, G, I'm woke."

He opened the door and walked into my room carrying a plate of food with a smile on his face which I returned. I pulled myself up to rest against the headboard.

"Aw, Goose, you didn't have to do this!"

He grabbed a book off my dresser, sat it in my lap, and then sat the plate on top of it.

"You know what it is, sis."

I looked down at the plate of food and smiled. He cooked me eggs, bacon, and pancakes with blueberries. Goose was crazy as shit, but he could cook. I hadn't had his cooking in months and missed it. He hadn't been around much, and when he was, his mood was all over the place. I could tell that now, he was in a great mood.

I scooped up a forkful of blueberry pancakes and stuffed them in my mouth. I closed my eyes, savoring the sweet taste of perfect pancakes.

"Mmmmh," I said with a smile before licking syrup off my lips. "I swear Goose, you need to consider cooking professionally."

Goose pulled my vanity chair up to the bed and crossed his arms over his chest, "Ain't nobody gone hire no killer."

"Who said anything about getting hired? Open your own restaurant, brother," I told him before biting into a piece of bacon.

He cocked his head a bit with a crooked smile, "I admire that about you, Ryann. You see the good in everything that's fucked up. You gone go places. You and my nephew. I pray to God the savage shit skips him like it skipped you." Goose stood up, kissed me on the top of his head and walked away chuckling, "Sis say open yo own restaurant." He then looked over his shoulder at me, "Aight Ry baby, enjoy the food. Holler if you need me."

"Okay Goose..."

He walked out of the room, and I could still hear him laughing. I wanted the best for my brothers, but they wanted the savage shit. Goose only viewed himself as a killer, but I knew there was more to him. He'd just rather embrace the bad. It wasn't like he had much of a choice though. Honestly, Goose was too unstable to run a restaurant, I just wanted him to know that he was more than just a murderer.

Chapter 11– Cass

She jumped back when she slid the shower curtain back and I was standing there. I had to grab her to stop her from falling.

"What the hell are you doing here?" Ryann yelled once she regained her composure.

"I came to apologize," I said as I helped her out of the shower.

Seeing her naked had thrown me off a lil' though. I wanted to be genuine with my apology because I wanted shorty to know that I meant the shit, but I couldn't help but want to taste her. She had put on a little weight, but it looked damn good on her. Her titties were a bit bigger, and her nipples were poking, begging me to put my lips on them.

I didn't realize I was staring until she sucked her teeth and said, "You sure you came to apologize, nigga? Standing there with ya dick all hard, I ain't heard an apology yet."

I chuckled and dragged my top teeth over my bottom lip, "My bad, love."

I passed her a towel hanging on the towel rack and she wrapped it around her body before shutting the lid to the toilet and sitting on it, "I mean... I get it, but damn."

She was in a joking mood and that made shit move a lot smoother. I just knew she was going to be frowning the whole time, considering the shit that's been going on between us two.

I rubbed my chin and sat across from her on the edge of the tub, "I apologize for not telling you about yo slut ass cousin, sweetheart. That shit happened before we happened—

"Don't matter."

"It does. I'm quite sure a few of the knucklehead niggas I got on payroll tried to get on you once upon a time. That nigga Loc... dawg seems reaaaal fond of you. I'm sure he tried you. You didn't tell me that... do I have the right to be mad?"

She shrugged and told me I had a poin,t but still felt like I should have told her since girl is her cousin. I understood where she was coming from too, so I didn't argue with that.

"And then this bitch told you about the abortion and you didn't even tell me."

I squinted and sucked my teeth, "Fuck you talm'bout? Somebody called and told me, but I didn't stay on the line with the bitch, asking for names and shit. They told me and hung up right after."

"Oh... well... it was her," she said as she dried off. "Can you hand me that lotion please?

I grabbed the bottle of Jergen's off the rack and squirted some into the palm of my hand. Standing in front of Ryann, I began to rub lotion onto her shoulders. She closed her eyes and let me touch her in ways I hadn't touched her in a while. Her butter soft skin felt good underneath my hands.

But then she opened her eyes, and snatched the bottle off the floor, "Thank you. I accept your apology... you can go now."

I was trying to put her pussy on my tongue. She knew what type of shit I was on and shut me down immediately. I found it hard to believe that shorty had been curving me as much as she had been. I remembered there was a point in time when Ryann could barely speak in my presence. Shit flipped and I was the blame.

After I dropped her off that day, I felt like shit afterwards. I couldn't believe I had spoken to her like that. I couldn't believe I sat there and let her cry knowing hurting her was the last thing I ever wanted to do. I always wanted to keep a smile on Ryann's face. She was too fucking beautiful to be frowning. Too fuckin beautiful to be crying over a nigga like me.

I hurt her. I pushed her away. And since then, she had been giving me the cold shoulder, barely speaking to me, not answering my texts… none of it. She was treating me the way I forced her to treat me and the shit was eating at my soul. I could have went about it another way. All I had to do was tell her the way I felt, but my pride got in the way.

I wanted to right my wrongs with her. But first, I needed to right the wrongs in my own fucked up life.

"I want to show you something," I told her, steady gawking as her titties, mouth salivating and all that.

I wanted shorty bad. My dick was stiff as fuck, so hard that it was starting to hurt. I unbuckled my belt buckled and she looked up at me with one of her eyebrows raised.

"Nigga, I know exactly what your dick looks like. Keep it in your pants."

I laughed and tossed my head back, "Fuck on, goofy. I want you to take a ride with me. A nigga ain't trying to show you dick."

She giggled, "Ohhh. Shit, I'm just saying," She goofily popped her lips like a hood rat and said. "Yeah, I'll ride with you, Cassim."

*

"What's this," she asked looking up at the building.

"A work in progress. But what it will be is a little piece of heaven for a kid going through hell," I said as I threw the car in park and unbuckled her seatbelt. "Come on. Let me share my vision with you."

She smiled, "This the group home, Cassim?"

I nodded and hopped out of the car. Ryann was the first person to come here outside of Scotty. Usually, I kept my shit a secret until business was afloat, but I wanted to share this with Ryann. She knew about it anyway.

I maneuvered to her side of the car and extended my open hand to her. She grabbed hold of my hand and I helped her out of the car, although she didn't need my help. I was looking for any chance to touch up on shorty. It wasn't like before, when I could just ease up behind her. I couldn't just reach out and touch her face like I used to. She'd flinch away and that was my fault. I didn't like the way she rejected me, so I made my touching seem innocent.

I grabbed her bag off the backseat and handed it to her before closing the door for her.

Ryann grabbed the bag from my hand and I extended my other hand for her to grab hold of. She looked down at it, and then back up at me.

"Hold my hand, Ryann," I pleaded.

She sighed, and finally placed her small hand into mine.

As I led her to the building, she looked up at it with a twinkle in her eye, and a smile spread wide across her beautiful face. Her smile… her greatest asset. The building was under construction, still going through the beginning stages, but you'd think it was completed by the smile on her face.

"This is amazing, Cassim."

She tried to pull her hand away from me, but I tightened my grip, not wanting her to let go. She didn't notice. Or at least she didn't seem to, because she didn't try to loosen her grip again.

"Yeah, it's still under construction, but this right here… will be my biggest accomplishment yet. I mean, aside from busting a nut in the dopest young woman in the world."

I was boasting, knowing fuck well that was a conversation I should have stayed away from. Especially since I was still a lil' hot about the abortion. I was just looking for any way to put a smile on her face. Or anyway to get some blushing up out of her. I wanted shit to feel like before.

Ryann sucked her teeth and playfully bumped into me, "Boy, don't gas."

I chuckled and ran my tongue over the corner of my mouth, "I'm just speaking facts though lil' baby." I fished around my pocket for the key to the building and said, "Everything has meaning to it now. Everything in my life serves a purpose. Everything I do from here on out, is about the blessing in your belly, ma."

Although I was being flirtatious, I was speaking true shit. For a minute, I was afraid of having a family. Always wanted it, but I feared what that meant for me. Having a family served as a weakness in the dope game. Niggas could never use the ones closest to me against me. I never had to worry about shit like mafuckas trying to take what was mine. The moment Ryann told me she was pregnant, I dropped down and pressed my ear against her stomach with thoughts of the what ifs floating through my mind. I was a lil paranoid but along with paranoia, lied hope.

Before Ryann...before the baby, I was just existing. Making money, simply living to die. Now I had purpose. Now I had something to live for.

Ryann looked up at me with that smile in her eyes but said nothing. I looked down at her with the same look. Unspoken words. Unspoken truths. I was opening up to her and she was pleased. Pleased with just a hint of sadness. Why couldn't I be this nigga with her right? Why couldn't I open up then? Why was I so withdrawn? I saw all of the questions through her eye contact.

But she said nothing.

I pushed the door to the building open and stepped inside.

"Keep an open mind for me real quick, sweetheart," I said as I extended my arms, gesturing for her to look at the building as a whole.

I then ran down every single plan I had for the group home. Ryann listened attentively, smiling, and nodding loving my vision. She offered advice and gave me a couple of pointers. Told me she would help as much as I wanted her to. She offered to help me start up the website. Said she would take photos and help me get it off the ground. Listening to her believe in my dream warmed my heart on some sucka shit.

Despite everything, Ryann was a solid ass woman. She could have been spiteful. She could have been evil. I mean, after all I did disrespect her and shut her out because she had an abortion. But she loved me through it all.

Staring at her, listening to her speak, I wished I could truly set my issues aside. I wanted her. But to take her now would be selfish. I knew I wasn't ready to move past what she did. I just wanted her because I needed her. She thought she needed me too, but right now... Cassim was the last person she needed in her life. She needed happiness.... She had to be healthy for the sake of our seed. If I took her into my arms right now, telling her I loved her and no longer gave a fuck about the abortion, I'd be lying.

"I think it'd be really dope to get some—what? What's wrong," she said, questioning the way I was looking at her.

"Nothing, sweetheart. Carry on," I said before, chewing on my bottom lip.

She let go of my hand and stood in front of me. She looked into my eyes and asked, "Cassim, are you alright?"

I nodded and ran my fingers over her cheeks, "I apologize."

"You already apologized—"

"I apologize for all of it," I said cutting her off.

I wanted to say that I apologized for not loving her the way she deserved to be loved. I wanted to tell her that I apologized for not listening. But I didn't.

"It's okay. *I've* moved past it," she said with a glare, adding much emphasis on the word I've.

"I'm trying," I said.

"Not hard enough. But that's neither here nor there. Let's not even get on that shit. We're vibing right now, let's just vibe."

*

After Ryann and I left the building, we grabbed something to eat and I dropped her back off. I wanted to spend more time with shorty, but Luck hit my line saying that he had some information to hit me with.

When I pulled up on Ryann's block, he was posted up with the other niggas waiting for me. I hopped out, grabbed Ryann's crutches from the backseat, and headed to her side of the car to let her out.

Once I helped her into the crib, I told her I loved her, and we parted ways. Shit had dead ass flipped. Before we fell out, baby would tell me she loved me every time we separated. Seemed like these days, I was the one who had to throw the first I love you out there.

When I got back to the whip, Luck was already sitting in on the passenger side. We slapped hands and he shook his head.

"What's the deal, fam," I asked, slightly annoyed with his silence.

"Shaneka Mosley," he said, locking eyes with me.

"Fuck is Shaneka? And what you mentioning her for?"

The fact that her last name was Mosley stood out to me, but I didn't know what the fuck he was name dropping her for.

"Shorty who went down to the station. Shaneka Mosely. Ryann's thot ass cousin."

I sat there, chewing on my bottom lip, rubbing the little stubble on my chin thinking. Bitch really had it out for a nigga huh?

"Damn, maybe I should've stuck dick to her, huh?" I joked. "Bitch is a true ass nutjob. Where you get that info from, G?"

Luck shifted around in his seat, with a shrug, "Snatched it up off Scotty. You say dawg wouldn't give you the name... so I masked up and ran down on 'eem. Stuck em up, snatched his file, got the fuck out of dodge. You wanted facts, you got facts, my nigga."

So Scotty had the name the whole time... I knew the nigga had been withholding information from me. I felt like a weight had been lifted off my shoulders though. If he would have told me it was Tiny, I would have offed her, despite the seed growing in her stomach. I was trying to be a better nigga, for the sake of my own child. But I still would have put a bullet straight through the middle of her head.

"You seen that bitch around here anywhere?" I asked looking up at Ryann's crib.

"Not since shorty went ape on her last night. Bitch probably got the fuck on. But you know me, and you know I'll find her."

I nodded, "I want the bitch breathing when you get her."

"I already know what it is fam. I know exactly what them type of hos get—The worst."

Chapter 12 – Ryann

Loc sat next to me and handed me my bowl of chocolate ice cream, "You straight?"

I grabbed the ice cream from him and nodded, "Yeah, you can turn the bottom lock on your way out."

He stood there with his hands stuffed into the front pockets of his designer jeans, "You sho? Can a nigga get a lil' smile or some shit, queen? You've been sitting on this couch with that same empty expression on your face since I got here."

I gave him a fake smile, "Yes, nigga. I am good."

"Aight now, don't make me have to fuck a nigga up over you."

I didn't find that cute, amusing, flattering or none of that shit. Although things with Cassim was rocky, I wasn't going to sit back and let Loc talk crazy about him. He didn't say Cassim's name, but that's who he was talking about. Our breakup wasn't a secret around these parts. And since my brothers knew I took shit like conflict between Cass and I to heart, they had Loc stopping by every other day to check up on me. Which was unnecessary.

"Chill out," I seriously said pointing my spoon at him. "I keep telling you niggas, whatever I go through with Cass is my business. I don't need babysitting, Loc."

He held his hands up, "Aight, queen. I'm just saying, baby. Give me word and its—"

"Buh-bye, Loc," I said pointing to the door. "Thanks for the junk food."

He nodded and told me to hit his line if I needed anything. He told me that same shit every time he left, but I never called him because I never needed anything from him. I wish Juice would dial back on the extra shit. He was only sending Loc over here because I didn't want to see his trif ass face.

I grabbed my phone and looked at the time. It was after midnight and the house was quiet with the exception of Jackie's loud ratchet ass yelling through the speakers of my new fifty inch TV. A lot of my time had been spent alone. Ashlee was moved out, probably staying with Juice on the low, and Shaneka was MIA since we fell out a week ago. Omni had been busy picking up extra hours at work, and Cassim...well... he came by every now and then. We hadn't spent much time together since he showed me what was going to be the group home.

I thought we were making progress. He had shown emotion, had apologized, and was a such a sweetheart. But then, like before, he began to pull away. I couldn't even say that he was playing with my heart at this point. I was the one with the unrealistic expectations.

I finished my ice cream off, and lied back on the couch, staring at the ceiling. I was merely existing now. I rarely smiled, because these days, I didn't have anything to smile about. The happiness had been sucked right out of me. I was coping with the reality I was forced to live in. I cried my last tear over Cassim. I was giving that man too much power. And it wasn't intentionally.

Do you think for one second that I truly wanted to love that man as much as I loved him? It just happened. And while I still love him, I was going through the detoxification process. I was learning to live without him. But what is life without really living it? I sat in this house all day, doing nothing but eating, watching, and thinking about him. I needed to get out.

I had been cooped up in this house for days now, but tomorrow, I planned on going out to take a few pictures, although photography wasn't the same for me anymore.

The front door opened and I said, "Loc, I said I was—

"Loc?"

I sat straight up and Cassim was closing the door, "You fucking with that nigga now?"

"What do you want," I said as I self-consciously ran my hands over my messy ponytail.

"I want you to answer your phone," he said as he sluggishly approached the couch where I was sitting at. "But shit, maybe you were too preoccupied with that nigga Loc to do so."

I waved him off, "Gone the fuck on somewhere. I'm not obligated to answer my phone for you, Cassim. You rarely call me as is. I haven't even seen much of you in the past three days. So, what are you popping up at my house for? Gone on back to doing whatever it was you been doing."

He grabbed my feet and began to massage them, with his eyes locked in on mine. He was quiet, but through his eye contact I could sense that something was wrong. And it wasn't the fact that I'd just mistook him for Loc. He had moved passed that, momentarily at least. It was something else. And knowing Cassim he wasn't going to tell me what is was.

I snatched my foot from his grip and stood up. I grabbed my melted bowl of ice cream and headed to the kitchen with him following behind me. I wouldn't dare look over my shoulder at him. I couldn't. Because, if I did, I would get lost in the black pearls located in the center of his eyes. I didn't want to get lost there. I didn't want to go down that road again. Staring into his eyes would only send me back down that dark road of addiction. Down that road of unrealistic expectations. Down the road of pain.

"Yo, what you on, sweetheart? I thought shit was smooth between us. That nigga Loc got you on a new level, huh?" he asked as he leaned up against the refrigerator with his arms crossed over his broad chest and a smirk on his face.

I huffed and shook my head as I ran water in the glass bowl, wanting to throw it at his face. But I wouldn't dare. To throw a glass bowl in his face would destroy one of God's greatest creations. The perfect face of Cassim.

"Nah. That nigga Cassim got me on a new level," I said as I shut the water off. "Fuck outta here with that goofy shit."

I was a completely different person than the one I was showing you. I showed you vulnerability. But I showed Cassim strength. The type of strength I've never been able to have when it came to him. The type of strength that was only brought on by pain. Pain caused by him. Pain that lied dormant in my soul, eating at me every day.

Everyday, I replayed that day in the car over and over again.

"That shit is dead." Those four words were a constant reminder. I did get caught up in him showing me his property, grabbing my hand and all of that. I always get caught up in him. But those four words reminded me why not to.

Cassim licked his lips and followed me out of the kitchen, "You walking around this bitch, prancing around that nigga with yo ass spilling out of your shorts on some true ass rat shit. You let that nigga beat—"

"Cassim get the fuck out of my house," I yelled.

I was so infuriated. I couldn't believe he was talking to me this way. There was obviously something wrong with him. And he had come over here just to fuck with me. But why? That shit dead ass hurt my feelings.

He sighed and ran both of his big hands down his face, "Fuck. Look, Ryann… my bad—

"I said get out!"

I didn't want to hear what he had to say. I just wanted him to go. He was bugging. Real life fucking bugging.

He ran his thick tongue over his bottom lip, nodded, and walked out of the house.

*

How did he get in my house?

I woke up to kisses on the nape of my neck, and the strong scent of Cassim. It was still dark outside, but the singing of the birds told me that it was early in the morning, but the sun hadn't awakened yet.

"Stop," I said as I tried to wiggle free from his strong grip.

Cassim wouldn't stop though. He kept his arms wrapped around me and his soft lips on my neck. He whispered an 'I love you' in my ear that I did not return. At first, I said I couldn't say that Cassim was playing with my heart. Because he wasn't. But now... now he was. And he was playing with it in the worst way possible.

Tugging at the vessels with every kiss he planted on my skin. Tugging at my hearts strings, like he was a puppeteer with every I love you spoken. He kept repeating himself. Professing his love for me in between kisses. Causing tears to stain the satin pillowcase underneath my head.

"I'm sorry," he said with his fingers on my chin, turning my head towards him.

His eyes twinkled under the moonlight, shining just a tinge of light on his truth. He was sorry, and he meant it.

"I'm sorry for hurting you. Sorry for not loving you. Sorry for everything, Ryann," he said before running his thumb over my lips.

I closed my eyes and I felt him sweep a tear from my cheek when he said, "Open your eyes."

I listened. Because although he'd hurt me, Cassim still controlled me. He still made my body do things against my will. My body wouldn't do what my mind told it to do. Not when I was under his spell. Not when he had his hands on me the way he did. Not when he was emotionally available. Cassim was almost never emotionally available. So, when he was, I fell victim of his love.

And when his hand landed on my inner thigh, a moan escaped my mouth. He'd sucked the air out of my lungs with the simplest touch. Except this time, I didn't have to be reminded to breath. He gave me air, when he pressed his mouth against mine. Parting my lips, he breathed into my mouth just before his tongue slow danced with mine.

Passion.

The passion I thought we lost. It was back. So much passion. There was so many unspoken words, being exchanged between the passion behind our kiss. His hand snaked around my head and he pulled me closer to him. Cassim kissed me harder than ever before. He kissed me like he meant it. Kissed me like he was dying of hunger and only my kisses could fill him.

That shit is dead.

Through our kiss, my subconscious spoke to me. I couldn't be weak. I couldn't lose my voice. I had to find it. Because if I lost it, I would lose my strength. Or had I lost it already? I couldn't give in to Cassim. Not with unfinished business. Not with those four words taunting me.

I pulled away from the kiss and moved away from his grip.

"Cassim... leave."

Cassim didn't move a muscle. He lied on his back, with his eyes on the ceiling, and his fingers interlock.

"I said leave—

"Just let me hold you, aight?"

The sadness behind his voice ate me up. I wanted to turn him away. I felt like I needed to. But I didn't want to neglect him. I didn't want him to feel the emptiness I felt because of his neglect. I wouldn't wish that pain on my worst enemy. I always wanted Cassim to feel my love, because he needed to. Because I needed him to. He didn't know what love truly was until he met me. Just as much as he needed to wrap his arms around me, I needed them wrapped around me as well.

He told me before that I could just call him for whatever, whenever, no matter the reason, but I didn't. The strength I was trying to build wouldn't allow me to. Now though, it seemed as if roles had been reversed. A man who never wanted to show weakness, as he called it, was showing it.

He was showing me that he needed me, so in return I showed him that I needed him too.

I lied next to him, with my back to him, and he wrapped his arms around me.

To feel his hot breath on the nape of my neck again, gave me such peace. To feel his strong hand rubbing against my belly, gave me butterflies.

"I do love you Ryann Marie Mosley. I never want this to die," he said against my earlobe.

I said nothing. I closed my eyes and drifted off to sleep.

*

The next morning, I woke up to him calling my name and touching my arm. I opened my eyes and Cassim was sitting on side of the bed, looking down at me.

"What are you doing today?" he asked with the sound of sleep still heavy in his voice.

"Pictures," I replied.

He leaned down, kissed me on my forehead, and stood up to leave. Before he walked out of the room, he looked over his shoulder at me and said, "I didn't mean any disrespect last night, sweetheart. A nigga just—"

I held my hand up, "It's okay. I'm okay. We're okay."

He nodded, steady staring at me.

He had more to say, but the only thing that left his lips was a sincere I love you.

I told him I loved him too and he walked out.

*

Silence.

The neighborhood was quiet, with the exception of the steady whistling of the wind. Fall was approaching, and school was starting, so the weather had gone from hot to cool. That little girl who'd often be standing on her porch waving when I headed to the field wasn't outside. The block was still, with the exception of the trees swaying, ridding themselves of the beautiful leaves spring had brought on.

I was smiling. Happy because fall was my favorite season. The beautiful hues of the leaves photographed beautifully. Outside of the great pictures I'd get, fall was the season for bomber jackets, straight leg jeans, cute boots, and scarves. I loved fall fashion.

I was happy. After Cassim left, I got up and showered. I didn't care that it was eight o'clock in the morning. I was eager to get my day started. I went down town and took a few pictures of the buildings, and the hustle and bustle too. I had me a cup of coffee and a bagel from Starbucks, and then I came back to the hood to take photos in my favorite spot

So far the day had been going well. Up until I heard her voice.

"Can I talk to you for a minute?"

I turned around and standing there fidgeting with her phone was Tiny. I hadn't seen her in a long time. I wondered, where the fuck had she been? And what was she doing showing her face in the hood, knowing everybody around here thought she was a rat.

My eyes immediately shifted down to her protruding belly and I wondered... was this bitch pregnant by Cassim too? He said they fucked right? I prayed like hell that she wasn't.

"What's up," I said with raised eyebrows.

She looked over her shoulder like someone was following her, "I just want you to know that I did not tell the police Cass killed Dinero's family."

Her voice was shaky and her top lip was quivering.

"Everybody think I did, but I didn't. I wanted somebody to blame and I have my speculations, but I would never go down to the precinct ratting," she paused and ran her hand over her hair, which was blowing wildly in the wind. "This shit is too much. Constantly looking over my shoulder, wondering if today is the day that I'm going to die. It's too stressful and stress is the last thing I need right now. I'm going through enough as is."

Why was she talking to me like I gave a fuck about the stress she was under?

"Who you pregnant by?" I asked, nodding towards her stomach.

My heart thumped rapidly as I waited for an answer. If this bitch said Cass, I would straight up lose it. I was going to hop right in the whip, and ride down on his black ass.

She looked over her shoulder again and then back at me, "Dinero."

I laughed. I literally cracked up laughing because bitch I was relieved. When it comes to Dinero and Tiny, I no longer gave a damn. It might have stung a little when I learned about their affair, but now I couldn't care less.

"Have you heard from—

"Bitch no. Fuck outta here, Tiny. You spoke ya lil piece... for what I don't know. You coming to me like I can control what the hell Cass does. Your best bet is to get the hell out of dodge. Even if you didn't do it. That matters none to a nigga like Cass. All that matters right now is what it looks like."

She stuffed her hands in the pocket of her PINK hoodie, nodded, and turned away.

Chapter 13- Cass

"Come outside," I said as I looked up at her house.

"For what? I'm lying down—"

"Get yo lazy ass up and come ride with me, sweetheart. That raggedy ass couch ain't going nowhere," I joked.

She sucked her teeth and laughed a little before she told me to wait a minute. Waiting a minute would turn into twenty, so I killed the engine and hopped out after we hung up.

A few nights ago, I let go of my ego, and climbed through her bedroom window like a real weirdo. I felt like I was losing baby. She hadn't answered any of my calls, and when I popped up on her, she thought I was Loc. I didn't like the way shit was going. I no longer wanted to push her away. I needed Ryann like I needed my next breath.

I jogged up on the porch and knocked on the door. Seconds later, she opened up dressed in an oversized shirt that looked hella familiar.

She covered the shirt, by wrapping her arms around her body, "I told you to give me minute—

I pulled the storm door open and walked right in, "You stealing niggas shirts and shit now? How much more of my shit you got up in here?"

Ryann rolled her eyes, "Boy, please. This is Goose shirt."

I pulled her arms away from her body to get a good look at the tee, and smirked, "Mine. It's aight though, shorty. I get it. But if you wanted to feel closer to me, all you had to do was hit me up. Shit, at least this time I would've been walking through the front door and not climbing windows."

"Creep! That's how you got in my house that night? Dawg, I gotta keep my shit locked up," she said shaking her head.

"You like me being a creep over you though, my baby. Keep it a stack," I said with a smirk.

She rolled her eyes again and headed towards her bedroom. I bit my bottom lip, watching her ass switch away in my t-shirt, wondering if she had on any panties. By the look of the jiggle of her ass with every step she took, she didn't.

"Where are we going?" asked Ryann as she looked around her closet for something t wear.

"Shopping," I replied, looking through the pictures in her camera I'd picked up from her dresser.

It was weird not seeing any pictures of me, as crazy as that may sound. I never liked it when she took pictures of me, but for some reason, not seeing any of me made me feel some type of way. It gave me that feeling that I was losing her again. I sat the camera down, and lied back on her bed.

"For what—"

"Stop asking questions. You riding with me, that's all that matters," I said as I watched her bend over to grab some shoes. "Thank God summer's over. A nigga might dead ass croak if I have to see those ratty ass Fenty slides."

She looked over her shoulder, "That lil' joke it getting played. I barely even wear those anymore."

Ryann was still giving me a hard time. This shit has been going on for weeks now. I thought she would be a little nicer after the other night, but she wasn't. I thought shorty would always be there, waiting around for me to get my shit together. But as time progressed, I realized that I was wrong.

I needed to sit down and talk to her about what happened before I truly did lose her. It was time for me to see shit from her point of view. Letting go was a must at this point. Ryann was slipping through my fingers like melted butter. I couldn't lose her. If I lost her, I'd lose it.

"Stop being so evil, with yo fat ass," I said, steady trying to lighten the mood.

"Only thing fat on me is this ass. Stop playing," she cockily said with a smirk.

"That ass and that pussy too, lil' baby," I said before dragging my top teeth over my bottom lip.

She blushed, but quickly dismissed it by slick talking, "My phat pussy ain't none of your concern, play boy."

"Aight Ryann... keep fronting like you won't take all of this dick if I offer it to you. I branded that pussy, sweetheart," I said as I stood up.

She looked over her shoulder and said, "You sure in the fuck are feeling yourself."

I stood behind her while she fingered through the clothes in her closet, looking for something to throw on. I stepped closer, pressing my body against hers, awaiting the reaction I always got when I did this to her. Anticipating the reaction I got last night. The labored breathing, the goosebumps that'd pop up on her arms, all of the shit that told the story of how much she loved me. But I got nothing. Even when I touched her, I got nothing.

Was shorty really gone? Had I truly pushed her to a point of no return?

She walked away from me, holding clothes, heading out of the room.

"I'm about to shower real quick, I won't be long."

I stood there, nodding with my hands stuffed in my pockets, lost. What happened? What the fuck just happened?

*

"What mall are we going to," asked Ryann with furrowed eyebrows. "Ain't nothing out this way."

"I never said we were going to the mall, sweetheart. I said shopping," I said as I glanced at her.

She pursed her lips together, "Mmhmm. Well, pass me the AUX cord. I cannot listen to another Meek Mill song. I'd die."

I laughed at her dramatics and unplugged my phone. She plugged hers up and started to dance in her seat to Signs by Drake.

Champagne with breakfast while I'm yawning
You can't drink all day if you don't start in the morning
Lord forgive me, I can't take things slowly (No)
I'm goin' on them once I get going (No-no)

She tryna take it all off for me
Tryna stay real close to me
I gotta catch myself
I can't play myself
I need to take it easy
Easy, easy, easy
Easy, easy, easy, easy

The whole ride, I let her control the radio. All I wanted to do was get in Ryann's good graces. I wanted her to respond to me the way she used to. I wanted her to look at me like she used to. Now the only thing I saw when she looked at me was pain. I hurt her, and it fucked with me heavy. I pushed her away, knowing fuck well I needed her in my life more than I needed air in my lungs. She *was* the air in my lungs. Without her, I'd fucking suffocate.

Thirty minutes later, she was asleep, and I was parking the car. I shut the engine off and unbuckled her seatbelt. I sat there, staring at her while she slept. Ryann did things to me that I couldn't explain. She made me feel like life was worth living. She made me feel like shit, fuck the abortion, fuck the fact that she kept that important information from me. Who was I to say she wasn't solid just because she didn't tell me? Who was I to push her away knowing fuck well that's the last thing I wanted to do? I needed her. Just as much as she had been addicted to me, I had become addicted to her.

Knowing this... would I be able to verbalize it? Would I be able to open up to her as she had opened up to me? I didn't like to be vulnerable. Vulnerability wasn't a good look on me. But for Ryann, I felt like fuck it. Let me gone ahead and pour my heart out to her.

She opened her eyes and I didn't move away. I lifted my arm and ran my hand over her butter soft skin. She closed her eyes and exhaled, with parted lips. Parted lips that reminded me of last night's kiss. Parted lips that made my dick rise. Damn. I inched in closer to her, and she moved away. I didn't have the same effect on her, and that was eating me the fuck up. No lie.

She grabbed the door handle and opened it.

I chuckled, in disbelief, as I unbuckled my own seat belt.

"I thought we were going shopping," said Ryann looking up at the house.

I hopped out and closed the door, "We are going shopping. House shopping."

She looked over at me as I made my way over to where she stood on the other side of the car, "Wait... what?"

"House number one of three. Come on. The realtor is waiting."

I was getting Ryann out of the hood. It was an absolute must. Regardless of what becomes of us, I had to get her out of Detroit. She was carrying my seed and I'd be damned if any of her brothers' shit ended up following them to her crib. Fuck no. I'd dead ass go ape shit.

She stood there, averting her eyes from me, and back to the mansion of a house. It was extra. Extra because baby deserved the absolute best. Both of them—her and the one growing inside of her.

"Cassim," she said in a low voice, my name sounding like a sweet hem falling from those sweet lips I missed.

"Say it again," I said, stepping closer to her.

She shook her head, backing away, "This is too much."

"No, it's not," I said with my hand extended. "Come on."

She looked down at my hand and shook her head, "I'm not going into that house with you. I'm not playing these games with you. I'm not a fuckin' toy Cassim. You cannot play with my feelings like this."

I sighed, hated the sadness in her eyes. Hating the sadness in her voice even more. I'd broken a woman I never wanted to break. I've given her love and ripped it right away.

"Ryann, please," I begged.

She thought I was begging her to come inside of the house with me. But I wasn't. I was begging her to love me the way she used to. I was begging her to forgive me. I wanted forgiveness. I wanted to grab shorty and to tell her everything I've been expressing to you. My pride was getting the best of me. Having feelings for women was foreign to me. Having to open up, and express love made me uncomfortable. I preferred to have walls up. But with Ryann, I pondered letting them down. If I didn't, I'd lose her. And if I lost her, I'd lose me. Didn't I say she was the fuckin' air in my lungs?

"I understand… you want me out of the hood. And I'm going to get out. Just on my own buck. Not like this," she said before turning away to get back into the car.

I grabbed her arm and pulled her into my chest. I held her tighter than ever before. I had that same fear I had after her accident. Like I was going to lose her. I didn't want to lose her. Why in the fuck couldn't she see that? Women want shit verbalized and all that. But shit, what happened to actions? Actions speak louder than words. Lately, by my actions, I'd been screaming 'I'M SORRY, SWEETHEART'. But she didn't give a fuck.

"You're crushing me," she struggled to say.

I let her go, lowered my head, and murmured, "I lost you?"

"What?" she asked as she adjusted her cut up sweatshirt.

I chewed on the corner of my lip and repeated myself.

She didn't say anything, but she did chuckle.

"Now you give a fuck, huh?" she asked, shaking her head.

"I've always given a fuck," I said with a frown.

"Have you? Really? Have you? Cassim you broke my fucking heart. You didn't give a fuck! *I* gave a fuck. I loved you with everything in me. When I say that shit, I mean that shit. I loved you with more than just me. *I loved you with my soul.* The love I had for you," she looked up to the sky shaking her head. "I couldn't even begin to truly describe it. Even if I did attempt to explain it to you, you still wouldn't know because there are no words that can thoroughly decipher it. No words to explain the feelings. No words to describe what loving you was to me. To love someone as much as I loved you?" She paused and ran her tongue over her bottom lip, "Is… toxic. Is…weak."

"Don't do this, shorty," I said, struggling to tap into my true feelings. "Stop doing this, Ry."

"What? Stop doing what? Stop doing to you what you've done to me," she asked with a frown. She walked away, heading for the car. "Take me home."

As I watched her walk away, my heart skipped a beat. Her walking away from me felt symbolic to her walking out of my life. I didn't want that.

I jogged up to her before she could get into the car. I grabbed her arm, forcing her to turn around, and when she did, I dropped down on my knees.

I held both of her hands in my hands and pulled her closer to me. Grabbing the back of her thighs, I rested the side of my face against her belly. She tried to pry my hands away from her, but I held on tighter.

I had never bowed down to anyone, but I was bowing to her. I needed her to know just how much I needed her. With shit like this? Life just wasn't right. Life hadn't been the same since I ended shit with her.

"Cassim—"

"Forgive me, sweetheart," I said, interrupting her.

"The realtor is watching," she whispered.

I didn't give a fuck about the realtor watching. I didn't give a fuck about the rest of the world. All I gave a fuck about right now was Ryann forgiving me. I needed her to give me a second chance.

"Forgive me—

"I forgive you. Now, get up," she said, steady trying to pull my arms away from her.

"Why do you keep trying to snatch away from me and shit, Ryann," I snapped. "Let me touch you. Let me hold you."

Ryann stopped trying to pull me away. She ran her hands through my dreads, letting me touch her… letting me hold her.

Chapter 14 – Ryann

Cassim was making me emotional. On top of the emotions I had because of the pregnancy, I was an emotional wreck.

"Come on, Cassim," I said after standing in the middle of the driveway with his arms wrapped around me and his head resting on my belly for about ten minutes now.

"Tell me," he said, wanting me to feed his ego the way I use to.

But I wasn't sure if I wanted to. I still felt the same way, but Cassim didn't deserve to hear the words he wanted to hear. He didn't deserve to be told 'I am yours'. Because right now, I wasn't.

"Ryann," he plead, looking up at me with sad eyes.

He was so sad. I didn't know what to do with him. I didn't know how to handle this Cassim. As I looked down at him, it was like looking into the eyes of a child. One who had been mistreated, neglected, and abandoned. It was because in a sense, I was.

I could see that Cassim still had issues. Issues of neglect and betrayal. At first, I thought he could have possibly been over his traumatic childhood. He was always so strong. The only time I witnessed him show emotion about it was when he would weep in his sleep. Never like this. All of this time, I had been dealing with a broken man.

"I need to hear it. I need to know—"

"I'm yours, Cassim."

"Every inch of you... all of you," he asked with his voice slightly muffled by my shirt.

I didn't say anything and he held me tighter, "Say it."

I looked away, as tears rolled down my face, "Yes, Cassim. All of me. I'm yours. Mind, body, and soul."

"What about your heart?"

I licked my lips and held his face in my hands, "My heart too, Cassim."

I just wanted him to stop. I wanted the sadness to stop. I needed him to stand up. I didn't like this side of Cassim. I didn't like the look in his eyes. The look of abandonment. I hated it. It broke my heart to see him like this.

"Please stand up," I begged.

He stood up and immediately wrapped his strong arms around me. I melted into his chest and closed my eyes, listening to the heavy beat of his heart.

"I'm ready to talk about it," he said.

"Hi," said the realtor, waving. "I don't know if you guys are still interested in the house—"

"Give us a minute, okay," I said before wiping tears from my face. "Come on, Cass... let's...let's talk baby."

He grabbed my hand and led me to the car. He gripped my hand like he never wanted to let me go. He opened the car door for me and I sat down. Shortly after, he climbed into the driver's seat, quiet.

"Cass—

"You probably think I'm a sucka ass nigga, huh?"

I frowned, "No. I think you're a man showing emotion. Emotions that make you human."

He nodded, "I just don't want to lose you. I feel like I'm losing you, and I don't want that. So, if I gotta be on sucka shit then so be it—"

"It's not sucka shit, Cassim. I need honesty. If you keep carrying on the way you're carrying on, you will lose me. If you don't tell me how you really feel, I will walk away. Not telling me the real is considered sucka shit. Letting me walk away from you knowing damn well you don't want me to is sucka shit. You've got it backwards, babe."

What is it with men and emotions? Why do they think that keeping shit bottled in is beneficial to either of us? A lot of niggas lose good women because of pride. Fuck pride. If you want someon,e let them know. We cannot read minds. We were blessed with a lot of superpowers, but unfortunately mindreading was not one of them.

"Understand that this is new to me, Ryann. Sometimes I say shit I don't mean because I'd rather keep what I really feel to myself. In an attempt not to hurt myself. I let go with you, because you showed me something different. You loved a nigga regardless. I ain't the finest, and I do a lot of fucked up shit, but you loved me. You called me weird shit like beautiful... took pictures of me... told me you loved me. Gave me all of you. You gave me more than my own ma did.

"I let down walls with you. Fell in love with you when I told myself I would never love anybody. I told myself I wouldn't trust a fuckin' soul because mafuckas lie and disappoint. I didn't see that in you. I saw the real. So, when I found out you had an abortion, the shit dead ass crushed me. I put all of my issues aside, and said fuck it, why not love this woman? She loves me. So I loved you. And then you betrayed that trust. It never was all about the baby. It was about the secret. I understand that you had an abortion because you didn't want to chance it being his. I get that. What I don't get is why you couldn't keep it one hundred with me? Why did I have to find out from someone other than the lady I loved?"

He narrowed his eyes at me and continued, ". I didn't know what real love was when I met you. Ryann, you are all I know. You are the reason my heart beats. You and our baby. I don't want to lose you. I can't lose you."

I reached over and wrapped my arms around his neck, hugging him. I understood now. All along, I thought he was upset because I had the abortion. I never looked at it from his point of view. All along, I wanted him to see things from my standpoint, but I wasn't viewing them from his. Maybe if Cassim would have been this open with me from the start, I would have understood. Maybe then I would have sympathized. But none of that mattered now. All that matter now was moving forward. All that mattered now was that he had finally opened up to me and that he was willing to move forward because he felt like he couldn't live without me. I completed him, just as much as he completed me.

"I can't lose you either," I said with a sigh. "I love you so much, Cassim."

"I love you too, sweetheart."

*

After spilling his heart out to me, we were finally ready to view the house. At last, I felt complete. I felt so much comfort in knowing that Cassim wanted me. Cassim had truly forgiven me, and we could move forward. Moving forward was all I've ever wanted... all we've ever wanted. We just had a few humps to get over first.

The realtor greeted us with a welcoming smile, and a firm handshake. I liked how she didn't inquire about the melt down the both of us had not too long ago. She was so professional.

"Sorry about that," said Cassim. "I know your time is valuable."

She waved him off, "It's absolutely fine. You've kept me quite busy for the day." She turned to me, "I'm Valorie. You must be Ryann. Cassim speaks highly of you."

I blushed and nodded, "I am she."

Finally, she opened the door and it was love at first sight. I thought Cassim's house was immaculate, but this was absolutely astounding. The foyer was huge, with marble flooring and a beautiful skylight. The ceilings were the tallest I'd ever seen. Looking up at the light fixtures, all I could think about was how Cassim would need a ladder to change the lightbulbs if any of them blew.

Anyway, the house was huge. Right off the foyer was a grand spiral staircase that led up to the second floor. Looking up the towering staircase, I could see that there was a balcony area, showcasing just a bit of the hallway. As I was looking up, Cassim asked if I wanted to go up first. I told him I'd rather check out the bottom half then make my way up.

The whole time Valorie showed up the house, Cassim kept a tight grip on my hand and a smile on his face. I don't think I'd ever saw him smile so much in my life. He was happy, and I was too. Things felt real now. We were looking at a house, setting up for our future. Not just our future, but the future of our child as well. This was the way it should have been all along. But nothing is perfect, and a few mishaps in a relationship gives it strength.

*

I didn't want to part ways, and neither did he. But he had business to tend to, and I had to start packing.

We were standing outside of his car, leaned up against it, kissing like two teenagers. His hands were all over me, and mine were all over him. I missed this so much.

He gripped my ass, and pulled me closer to him, despite that I was already pressed against him.

"How long are you going to be," I said him before kissing him on the lips again.

"I don't know, beautiful. Hopefully not long. A nigga is dead ass trying to stick dick to you. Dick been dry for about two and a half months, so don't expect a nigga to last long."

I cracked up laughing, "Nigga you don't last that long anyway."

"I make that mafucka cream though, don't I," he said before lightly biting my earlobe.

"Mmhmm," I said, getting turned on by his nasty talk.

As fucked up as it might sound, I missed the dick more than I missed anything else. His dick fed my fucking soul. I was in dire need of it. Every night, I fell asleep yearning for it.

"Come fuck me," I said before grabbing his dick.

He grabbed my wrist and said, "I want to do more than just fuck you, sweetheart. I want to feast on you until you beg me to bend you over. I want to run my tongue from the crack of your ass—

"What up G? What's the deal," said Wavy walking up behind us.

I sucked my teeth and rolled my eyes, "Damn Wavy—

"The fuck wrong with you, nigga," snapped Cassim, moving me aside.

"My bad G. I just thought—"

"You didn't think. You couldn't have thought if you rolled up on me talm'bout 'What's the deal', when you see me conversing with my shorty. Fuck... Yo peoples didn't teach you any manners?"

I grabbed Cassim, turned his head in my direction, and whispered, "Calm down. It's not that serious. Go take care of your shit. I'll be here. I'm not going anywhere."

*

Cassim was gone, and I was dancing around the house, packing. Rihanna's Wild Thoughts was blasting through my speakers giving me life!

I don't know if you could take it
Know you wanna see me nakey, nakey, naked
I wanna be your baby, baby, baby
Spinning and it's wet just like it came from Maytag
White girl wasted on that brown liquor

When I get like this I can't be around you
I'm too lit to dim down a notch
'Cause I could name some thangs that I'm gon' do

I was busy folding clothes when I felt a presence behind me. I quickly turned around, and jumped at the sight of Omniel, standing there with tears pouring down her face, breathing heavily. I snatched the remote control to the sound bar off the table and immediately cut the music off.

"What's wrong, Omni," I yelled as I wrapped my arms around her.

I had a good idea of what was wrong. She had obviously found out about Juice and Ashlee. What else would have her crying the way she was crying? Devastation was heavy in her eye contact. She stood there with wide eyes, and shock plastered on her face.

"Jus—Justice and...and LeeLee. I caught them in bed together," she managed to say through the heavy crying she was doing.

I just held her tighter, while her arms laid flat to her sides.

"I'm so sorry Omni... so Sorry."

Through her sobs, she told me about how she left work early because she wanted to surprise Juice with something special. They had been doing good and he had been keeping a smile on her face, so she wanted to show some appreciation. But when she walked into the house, she heard moaning. What she didn't expect was for the moans to be coming from Ashlee.

What the fuck is wrong with them? At this point, I was really curious. I really wanted to know why they were fucking each other like there was nothing wrong with it.

SLAM!

The sound of my front door slamming made the both of us flinch. I looked up away from Omni, and Juice was coming our way with a deep scowl on his face.

I pointed to the front door, "Get the fuck out, Juice!"

He ignored me and grabbed Omni by her arm, "Bitch say that shit you just said to me before you left, again. I want to hear you say it again."

Omniel held her head high and said, "I'm telling everybody! Every got damn body about the way you fucked your cousin in our bed!"

"Let her go, Juice," I yelled, trying to pry his hand away from her small arm.

He then grabbed both of her arms and lifted her from her feet. I gasped when he threw her clean across the room. She flew across the room and went crashing down on top of my glass dining room table.

I charged at Juice, beating him in his back as he approached Omni who laid motionless on top of shattered glass, with his fist balled. It was like Juice was another person. His face was screwed up into a deeper scowl than before. He stood over Omni and wrapped his hands around her neck. She was already unconscious. What more did he fucking want? He wanted to kill her because she found out about his sick ass secret. Why not kill his mothafuckin self?

Fighting him was pointless. So, I marched away heading for my room where my gun sat comfortably in the top drawer of my nightstand. I would never kill my brother, but I needed to scare him away from Omni. I had to. If I didn't he would kill her.

After I left the room, I cocked the gun back and pressed it to the back of his head, "Get off of her, Juice."

Without a second thought, he elbowed me in my stomach, causing me to stumble back across the room. I tripped over one of my suitcases, and went crashing to the floor. Juice? He didn't check on me. He didn't even look over his shoulder to see if I was okay. He went right back to choking Omni.

I crawled towards the middle of the floor, where my gun sat, ready to really put hot lead through his sick ass. But before I could grab the gun, Ashlee came out of nowhere and snatched it up before I could.

She aimed it at me with shaky hands and tears pouring from her eyes, "Get back! Get the fuck back!"

I slid back, hitting the wall behind me with my hands up, as I stared down the barrel of my own gun. My heart beat crazy against my chest, as fear paralyzed me. A gun in my face. History repeating itself. Except this time, I was the one staring down the barrel of a gun. Not my mother. Was this the way I was going to die? The same way she did? The same way both my parents did?

I lowered my hands, and placed them over my stomach, crying.

My baby didn't stand a chance. We didn't stand a chance. If Ashlee killed me, she would kill the both of us. Did Ashlee care? Maybe she did... maybe she didn't.

I got my answer when she pulled the trigger.

BLAH!

Chapter 15 – Cass

"Where you find her at," I asked Luck as we walked through the old abandoned apartment building, you and I first met. The night I shot Keys in the hand at.

"Mocospace. On some slut shit, trying to fuck for cash," said Luck.

I shook my head as I entered the area she was in.

She was sitting in the middle of the floor, tied to a chair, gagged with tears and snot running down her face.

I stood in front of her and kneeled before snatching the gag out of her mouth.

"Help," she screamed like someone would really hear her.

I cupped my hands over my mouth and yelled with her, "Help! Help her! I'm about to dead this bitch! If you hear me, come help her!"

Luck laughed, standing on the other side of the room, "Yo, you wild bruh. Listen, Yasmin came through with that info too. I got the footage—

"Is the face visible? The license plate number? I need all of that, G. Today is my lucky fucking day."

God was pouring down blessings today, wasn't he? Shit was perfect with Ryann and I. We were getting ready to move into a crib that was shitting on the white mafuckas in my community, and Luck had found her slut ass cousin. Same bitch who tried to break us up… same bitch who tried to get me thrown under the jail too. Now bruh was telling me his lil' slut ass side bitch had footage of the ignorant fuck who had hit Ryann. I mean, shit. Life was being good to me. Damn good to me.

"Copy that, cuz. You already know I'm on it." He paused and pointed at Shaneka "How long you gone be at it with this one?"

"Not long," I said before pulling my banger from my waistband and pressing it against the middle of her forehead.

"Please... please don't," she cried.

"Ask God for forgiveness, Shaneka," I said before cocking the gun back.

"Please—

"I'm trying to look out for you, shorty. Tryna save you from eternal damnation and all 'lat. Ask 'em."

"I... I'm sorry—

"Fuck it," I said before I pulled the trigger, sending hot lead ripping through her cranium.

Her head fell back off impact. The bullet ripped through her shit so vicious that you could see the floor through the hole the bullet left.

I stuffed my burner back into my waistband and turned to leave, "Get one of them stupid niggas to get rid of her—

"Fuck," said Luck with raised eyebrows, staring down at his phone.

"What? What's the issue," I asked with furrowed eyebrows, wondering what the hell he had just found out that had him looking as vexed as he was looking.

Luck took a deep breath before turning his phone to face me, "What you wanna do with that info?"

I narrowed my eyes at face on his phone, as anger sat in.

"Bury it. Don't mention it. Ever. This stays between us," I said with tight lips.

"We gone handle it—

"It's going to be handled. But she's been hurt enough. We gone handle it, but don't speak of this shit ever again."

What the fuck is it with the people in Ryann's life deliberately hurting her?

"How you wanna handle it," asked Luck as we walked out of the apartment building.

I shrugged, as anger switched over to sadness. Or sympathy I should say. Ryann didn't deserve any of the fucked up shit that had been forced upon her. She had a mean streak, she could talk shit. But her heart was pure. She loved hard and did right by mafuckas.

"Make it look accidental," I said as I got into my car. "I'm about to go grab shorty. Find out what the location looking like and handle it."

"You don't want parts," asked Luck with raised eyebrows.

I turned the corners of my mouth up and shook my head, "Nah G. I'm about to go grab shorty. Right now, all I want to do is love her, my nigga."

He nodded, "I feel you, bro. I'ma handle that bitch in the building, then I'ma handle the other shit. I got chu."

I nodded, saluted Luck, and hopped in the whip.

That's all I wanted to do. I wanted to give Ryann the rawest, truest form of love possible. I wanted to love her the same way she loved me. She was getting one hundred percent of me, and not just because the people in her life were grade a fucked up. But because she deserved it.

*

When I pulled up on the block, it was flooded with squad cars. They had the block so sewed up that I had to park way at the other end of the block.

"The fuck these stupid ass, incompetent ass niggas do now?" I said as I unbuckled my seatbelt.

I grabbed my phone from the middle compartment of the car and dialed Luck up. He answered almost immediately, "What's good fam?"

"Everything smooth at the house? Block flooded as fuck right now," I said as I got out of the car and started down the block.

"Yeah, nobody's hit me up. Where they at?"

I didn't say anything. I dropped my phone and took off running down the block, heart beating heavy against my chest. The block wasn't flooded with cop cars because of the trap. It was flooded with cop cars because of something that had happened at Ryann's house.

When I saw the coroner's van turn the corner, I slowed my pace.

Was I too late? Just earlier, I was talking about how I had to get shorty out of the hood because I didn't want her brothers shit to fall back on her. Was that what had happened? Or did the mothafucka who hit her decide to finish her off another way? Since the hit and run didn't take her out?

I dragged my hands down my face, getting closer and closer to her crib. I had never been afraid of shit in my life. Well, not in my adult years. But right now, I was scared to take another step. I let my feet drag, as I headed down the block, now only three houses down.

The coroners headed up the steps, and cops spilled out of the house.

"Yo, what's good Boss? It's hot as fuck around these parts. Niggas scattered like—"

I pushed the young nigga who had rolled up on his bike away from me. He went crashing onto the ground in front of me, and I stepped right over him.

A few feet away, Goose and Adrien jumped out of a car, and treaded towards the house. I started to yell out, asking if Ryann was aight, but I decided against it. I wasn't prepared for what their responses would be.

I thought about turning away and heading back for my car. I felt like it would be in my best interest if I did. Because if I found out that it was Ryann them coroners were there for, I'd lose my mind. Losing her would mean I loss both of them. The only ones that made life worth living.

I wasn't ready to face reality. I felt like a coward, getting ready to turn away. But fuck it. I would have to just find out some other way. To be faced with the shit… it was just too much.

I chewed on my bottom lip and turned away.

"Cass!"

I took in a deep breath and turned around. She took off running towards me, crying, with a face full of tears. I wrapped my arms around her on impact, relieved.

"I thought I lost you," I said as I picked her up.

She wrapped her arms around my neck, and her legs around my waist then said, "LeeLee killed Juice."

I let her cry in my arms over a nigga who tried to murk her a month ago. I let her mourn his death because to tell her that he was behind the wheel of the car that hit her would crush her. I didn't want to hurt her more than she already was. So, I let her. I let her cry tears over a ho nigga who wanted her dead.

Ryann lied her head on my shoulder, crying quiet tears like we were the only people on the block. She lied there, quiet, in shock, while her brother was carried out of her house in a body bag.

*

I sat behind the wheel of the car, watching Ryann talk with Adrien and Goose, wondering how they would feel if they knew Juice was the one who tried to kill their beloved sister. I wondered if they would be mourning the ho nigga still.

My phone rang and I answered it.

"What's good, fam," I answered with my eyes still locked in on Ryann.

I watched her, wondering why the fuck her brother tried to take her out. Them niggas worshipped the ground Ryann walked on. There was nothing they wouldn't do in her honor. But Juice ran her down. He didn't give a single fuck neither. Couldn't have. To do her like that, and just ride off like nothing happened? Dawg couldn't have gave a fuck about her. But why? What did Ryann do to deserve that shit?

"I'm about to swing around the way to handle that one thing—

"Don't even worry about it fam. It's a wrap. It's been handled already."

I wanted the nigga Juice dead. That's it. How it happened didn't matter. I just wanted the snakes away from my queen.

Chapter 16 – Ryann

One Year Later

I hummed as I ran my hand over her soft, curly hair, slowly rocking back and forth in a rocking chair, trying to get her back to sleep. It was after three in the morning, and mommy was exhausted.

Riley had been getting up every hour, trying to get me to lie her in bed with us. But I wouldn't do it. We napped together every now and then, but I would never sleep through the night with her in bed with Cassim and I. It was too scary. So, if my fear of either of us rolling over her tiny self meant sleepless nights, then so be it.

A year had passed, and Riley Justice Mosley was two months old.

Riley was a Mosley because Cassim was uncomfortable with giving her his last name. He refused to give her a name he didn't feel that he truly owned. I tried to get him to speak to his mother, but he refused to. So, I didn't force him. But he did take a DNA test, which told him that he had Haitian roots. To me, just to get a DNA test wasn't enough. I wanted more, but Cassim was fine with that, so I left it alone. I prayed that one day, he would be open to actually sitting down with his mother just to truly move forward.

I gave her Justice as a middle name, in remembrance of Juice. Juice and I bumped heads, and he did a lot of shit I didn't approve of, but at the end of the day, he was my brother and I missed him. Some nights, I still dreamt about that horrible day. The day Ashlee killed him, right in front of me.

I thought she was going to kill me, but instead she quickly turned the gun on Juice and pulled the trigger. I sat there, against the wall, trembling, with bucked eyes, watching blood leak from the back of my brother's head while he lied on top of Omniel, dead.

Omniel was fine and had moved on with her life. She was finally happy too, and I was happy for her because she deserved it. She didn't regain consciousness until she was in the hospital recovering with broken bones as a result of Juice throwing her on top of the table. She woke up in shock. I couldn't tell if she was devastated about Juice's death or if she was still devastated about Juice and Ashlee fucking. Luckily, she didn't have to relive what happened like I had to every day.

Those horrible images would forever be embedded in my memory. And in Ashlee's too. After she killed him, she lost her mind. I couldn't understand why she killed him. And would probably never know the story behind it since she lost her mind. She just kept repeating that he deserved it.

Ashlee was never the same after she killed Justice. Right after she pulled the trigger, she dropped the gun, and began to laugh hysterically with tears pouring from her eyes, pulling at her hair, and scratching at her skin. She screamed about how 'it' was Juice and he deserved it. She was put in a mental facility, where she was her safest. She was better off there because Goose crazy ass wanted her head—literally.

As far as Shaneka goes, it was almost as if she had fallen off the face of the earth. I hadn't seen her and I didn't give one solid fuck. Her family had been searching high and low for her thot ass too. But me? I couldn't give a fuck less about her whereabouts.

I was happy and officially drama free. I was still in the process of building my photography company, but things were moving along just fine. I was satisfied with the progress because I knew that the best was yet to come.

I wasn't the only one happy. Cassim was smiling more these days. His group home had just finished its renovations and was due to be open for business within the next month or so. He was still heavy in the dope game but let Luck handle most of the work. Cassim spent the majority of his time with Riley and me.

Once Riley fell asleep, I lied her down and crept next door where Cassim and I slept. As soon as I crawled into bed with him, he wrapped his arms around me. I closed my eyes and lightly moaned.

I was still deeply in love with this man. Still I loved everything about him. I loved him more now than I did when I first fell in love with him. What Sinn said about eventually hating the sight of him was false around here. I could never hate the sight of him. The sight of him still gave me butterflies. At times, the sight of him still made me lose my voice. At times, I still got chills, and had to remind myself to breathe. Nothing had changed. Except now, I simply loved him more. I was truly addicted to Cass. I was a fiend for his love and there was no changing that. Cassim was made for me, and I for him.

"Next time, let her cry herself back to sleep. I'm tired of you leaving me," he said against the nape of my neck.

I laughed and playfully hit him on top of his hand, "No mean ass. I always come back, don't I."

He mumbled, "Mmhmm."

I turned around to face him and rubbed my nose against his, giving him an Eskimo kiss. Cassim opened his eyes and made eye contact with me. He moved closer to me, with his lips pressed against mine. He then let me go and ran his hand over my face. I closed my eyes and kissed his fingertips when they met my lips.

"Marry me."

I opened my eyes and moved his fingers away from my lips, "What?"

He grabbed me, sitting me on top of him, "I said, marry me."

It wasn't the most romantic way to ask, but did I give a fuck? No, I did not. Cassim could have taken me down to the court house, dressed in pajamas, with a bonnet on my head and said to me the same thing he just said, and I would still tell him yes.

I didn't give a fuck about the mushy stuff most women cared about. I cared about the love we shared. I cared about the way he made me feel. The way he asked me to marry him bothered me none. While most bitches trip about a man not getting down on one knee, I was fine with it. I didn't have a 'get down on one knee' type of man. I had a 'marry me' type of man. And I was perfectly fine with that.

"Okay," I said with a huge smile on my face. "I'll marry you, Cassim."

He reached up, grabbed the sides of my face, and pulled me closer to him. He pressed his dry lips against mine, and tongue kissed me with sleep still heavy on his breath. Did I care at all about the tart smell of his breath? No. All I cared about was Cassim. All I cared about was the fact that we had survived.

After all of the trials and tribulations we've gone through, all I wanted to do was be his wife. And even if he hadn't asked me to marry him, I still would be the happiest woman in the world because I had him.

At first, I never thought it was possible. But Cassim had crept into my crosshairs and showed me that I could indeed fall in love with a dope boy.

The End

** This isn't the end of Ryann and Cassim, but rather
The end of how Ryann fell in love with a dope boy.
There will be more of
Ryann and Cassim—just at a later date. I'm not ready to let
My baby's go just yet! **
Thank you for reading.
Please subscribe to my mailing list @
www.authormisscandice.com
And follow me on all social networks.
Facebook: Author Miss'Candice
IG: authormisscandice_xo
Twitter: MissCandice_xo

CPSIA information can be obtained
at www.ICGtesting.com
Printed in the USA
LVHW03s0206130718
583547LV00001B/57/P

9 781720 580362